The Plant
That Ate Dirty Socks
Gets A Girlfriend

Other Avon Camelot Books by
Nancy McArthur

THE PLANT THAT ATE DIRTY SOCKS
THE RETURN OF THE PLANT THAT ATE DIRTY SOCKS
THE ESCAPE OF THE PLANT THAT ATE DIRTY SOCKS
THE SECRET OF THE PLANT THAT ATE DIRTY SOCKS
MORE ADVENTURES OF THE PLANT THAT ATE DIRTY SOCKS
THE PLANT THAT ATE DIRTY SOCKS GOES UP IN SPACE
THE MYSTERY OF THE PLANT THAT ATE DIRTY SOCKS

NANCY McARTHUR lives in Berea, Ohio, a suburb of Cleveland. She teaches journalism part-time at Baldwin-Wallace College. She has a lot of plants, but none of them has eaten anything—so far. This is the eighth book about Michael, Norman, Stanley, and Fluffy.

The Plant
That Ate Dirty Socks
Gets A Girlfriend

Nancy McArthur

AN AVON CAMELOT BOOK

AVON BOOKS
A division of
The Hearst Corporation
1350 Avenue of the Americas
New York, New York 10019

Copyright © 1997 by Nancy McArthur
Published by arrangement with the author
Visit our website at http://AvonBooks.com
Library of Congress Catalog Card Number: 96-95086
ISBN: 0-380-78319-3
RL: 5.1

First Avon Camelot Printing: June 1997

CAMELOT TRADEMARK REG. U.S. PAT. OFF. AND IN OTHER COUNTRIES, MARCA REGISTRADA, HECHO EN U.S.A.

Printed in the U.S.A.

OPM   10   9   8   7   6   5   4   3   2   1

To the many readers
who asked for a girlfriend plant:
thanks for getting me started
on thinking about this possibility.

Special thanks to: Susan McArthur; Barbara McArthur; John McArthur; Sue Kennel Hall; Colin Evans and Jamie Evans, students at Fairwood School, Berea, Ohio; Jean Evans; Beth DiVencenzo's 1995–96 fifth graders at Brush School, Grafton, Ohio; Forest Graham and James Osborn, students at Hambden Elementary School, Chardon, Ohio; Erin Klayman and Brian Waldmener, students at Fairfax Elementary School, Mentor, Ohio; Jonathan Wilhelm; Joel Tourtelotte; and Anna Baltputnis and her fourth-grade classmates at Damascus Elementary.

The Plant
That Ate Dirty Socks
Gets A Girlfriend

Chapter 1

"Hi! Yah!" The yell startled Michael out of deep sleep. He heard a small crash, an "Oops," and a thud on the rug. This commotion had to be caused by his younger brother, Norman. Although Michael wanted to sleep a little longer, he opened his eyes to see what the expert pest was up to now.

In the morning sunlight from the window between their beds, Norman was being helped up off the floor by a couple of vines belonging to his almost six-foot-tall pet plant, Fluffy. Another vine picked up Norman's broken bedside lamp and put it back on his side of the wide bureau under the window. Norman was a neatness nut, and his plant had grown to be a lot like him. Next to Michael's bed, his own slightly larger pet plant, Stanley, stood motionless, ignoring what was going on.

"What are you doing?" asked Michael.

"Karate," replied Norman.

"But you don't know how. Your lessons haven't even started yet."

Norman said, "I saw karate movies. Over at Bob's. See?" He kicked one leg sideways so high that he started to topple over again. Fluffy's vines caught him before he hit the floor.

Michael said, "Too bad you can't take Fluffy along to your lessons to keep you from falling down."

Norman glared at him. He said huffily, "When Bob and I go to karate, I'm going to teach Fluffy everything I learn." Norman kicked again, lower this time. Fluffy reached out, but Norman did not tip over.

Michael sighed. There had been big problems after Norman taught the plants to do the Hokey Pokey. Karate would surely lead to disaster.

Mom came in, looking sleepy in her purple bathrobe. "Now what!" she said. "I heard a yell and a little crash."

"I was just practicing karate," explained Norman. "I sort of accidentally knocked my lamp over."

"Wait till you start your lessons so you can do it safely," ordered Mom. "Remember, when we signed you up, the teacher said karate's for self-defense, not attacking—and that includes the furniture." She unplugged the lamp. It was broken into several pieces.

Dad came in buttoning his shirt. "What happened?" he asked.

"Karate," said Mom. "Norman couldn't wait for his lessons. Do you think this lamp can be fixed?"

"It looks like a goner," he replied. "Come on," he told the boys. "Get moving, so you don't have to rush to get ready for school."

2

Norman was always up before anyone else, so he was raring to go. But Michael was a slow starter in the morning. He slid out of bed and tripped over a dirty sock left on the rug. Stanley had eaten only three of the four that Michael had put out last night for his dinner. Michael had discovered by experimenting that when the plants got more sunlight, they ate fewer socks in the middle of the night. He had taken Stanley out in the backyard for a while yesterday.

He asked Norman, "How many clean socks did Fluffy eat last night?"

"Four," said Norman. "Why didn't Stanley eat all of his? You're not going to leave that smelly sock there all day, are you? It'll stink up the whole room!"

Michael sealed the leftover sock in a plastic bag to keep it yummy for Stanley to eat later. He would rather put out too many socks than not enough. If the plants didn't get enough to eat, there was no telling what they would do. They were fastened to skateboards so they could be moved easily, but they had learned to pull themselves around with their vines. Once they had gone after orange juice in the refrigerator and made a giant mess.

As Michael brushed his teeth, he wished he could go back to bed. He had been up late reading with a flashlight under the covers because he couldn't wait to find out what happened next in *The Ghost of Creep Castle*. He yawned and went down the hall to the kitchen.

At the table he rested his head on one hand and shoveled cereal into his mouth with the other.

Mom said, "Your chin's almost in your cereal bowl. Do you feel all right?"

3

"I'm just sleepy," he mumbled with his mouth full. When he finished eating, he folded his arms on the table and put his head down.

"Wake me up when it's time to go to school," he said.

Dad said, "It's important to get enough sleep. If you're this tired, obviously you didn't. Maybe you'd better start going to bed half an hour earlier."

"No!" protested Michael, sitting up straight.

Mom looked at him suspiciously. "Were you reading with your flashlight under the covers again?"

"Uh, sort of. Just a little while."

"Tonight when you go to bed," said Mom, "I want you to hand over your flashlight."

"No."

"Yes," she said. "No arguing. What are you doing in school today?"

"Owl pellets," said Michael. "For science we're picking them apart to find bones of little animals the owls ate."

Norman stopped drinking his orange juice. "Oooh, yuck!" he exclaimed.

Mom made a face and asked, "Are those pellets what I think they are?"

Michael explained, "No. Mrs. Black said the owls cough them up."

"Owl vomit," said Norman. "Double yuck."

"Not exactly," said Michael. "It's the parts they don't digest, with fur and feathers. Like hair balls that cats hawk up."

Dad said, "Do you have to tell us about this while we're eating?"

4

Michael shrugged and grinned. "Mom asked."

"Aren't the pellets germy?" asked Mom. "Are you going to wear gloves?"

"No," said Michael. "Mrs. Black said the company that sells them to schools fixes them to be non-germy for picking through with bare fingers."

"Triple yuck," said Norman.

Mom said, "Wash your hands afterward anyway. Remember, after school we're taking Stanley and Fluffy to a plant place to get bigger pots and new soil. Don't dawdle on the way home."

Dad asked her, "Are you sure you don't want to wait till Saturday when I can go along to help?"

"The plants are easy to roll on their skateboards," she replied. "The boys and I can handle it. The place is only about a mile from here. It'll be a nice walk."

She added, "On Saturday, we could take a day-trip somewhere. I wonder if the new rain forest exhibit at the Elmville Zoo is open yet."

"I don't think so," said Dad. "There would have been something about it in the newspaper and on TV. But it seems like it should be open soon." He picked up the newspaper. "Hmmm. Some vandalism was discovered at the park yesterday. Spray paint. Broken benches. What kind of idiots do things like that?"

"Mean ones," said Norman.

"Isn't there any *good* news?" asked Mom.

Dad turned the page. "Here's some plant news. All the local plant clubs are getting together to hold an auction sale. They're raising money to create gardens for children in the park."

"Good idea," said Mom. "What are they selling?"

5

"Rare plants donated by club members and professional growers," Dad read. "And our good neighbor, Barbara Smith, is one of the chairmen."

"Can we go?" asked Michael. "It'd be cool to see rare plants."

Dad replied, "We already have two rare ones that you see all the time."

Mom suggested, "We could donate *them* to the sale."

The boys shouted, "No!"

"Just kidding," she said. "We won't go back on our deal to keep them."

Norman carried his cereal bowl, juice glass, and spoon to the sink. He neatly rinsed and stacked them. He was all ready for school, clothes looking nice, hair combed. His backpack sat by the kitchen door with everything he needed already in it.

Michael shoved his dishes into the sink with the bowl atop the glass. They tipped over with a clatter.

As Norman went out the back door to get his bike, he was singing "Oh Susanna," hitting wrong notes as usual. He loved to sing. He was always cheerful and organized in the morning. Michael wondered if Norman did it on purpose to drive him crazy. It was hard to live with someone who kept acting so perfect.

Mom reminded Michael, "Tuck in the other side of your shirt. Tie your shoelaces. And comb your hair. Why do I have to keep telling you these things every morning?"

Michael sighed and raked his fingers through his hair. While he tied his shoes, he tried to remember where he had put his homework. After a frantic search, it turned out to be in his backpack. He grabbed his jacket and

6

opened the back door to go get his bike from the garage. Mom handed him his milk money and lunch, which he had left on the sink.

"Your shirt's still hanging out," called Mom. "Tuck it in. Have a good day!"

The ride to school in the cold fresh air made Michael feel wide awake. When he went around to the back of the building, where the bike racks were, he saw a police car. The custodian, Mr. Jones, was talking to two officers. Michael recognized one. He was known as Officer Tim to everyone at Edison Elementary. He often visited classrooms to talk to kids about how to stay out of trouble. Michael and Norman had gotten to know him well when they had been mixed up in a mystery. As Michael got closer, he saw why the police were there.

Chapter 2

The playground was littered with broken glass. Purple and yellow paint had been sprayed all over. Kids stood around looking at the mess. The principal, Mr. Leedy, was rounding them up and sending them into the building.

"Who did this?" Michael asked Mr. Leedy.

"Fools who want to spoil things for others," replied the principal. "The police said it looks like the same ones who vandalized the park."

Mr. Jones came up. "I'll have all the glass cleaned up long before recess," he told Mr. Leedy. "And I should have a crew here to clean off the paint by later this afternoon. Whoever did this should be made to pay for the cleanup."

"After we catch them," said Officer Tim, "a judge will probably make sure of that."

In the halls and classrooms, everyone was talking

8

about the vandalism. Kids were angry that someone had done that to their playground.

After the pledge and announcements on the PA, Michael's class settled down to work on the owl pellets.

Mrs. Black passed out diagrams of the bones of the little animals that owls eat—mice, voles, or shrews—to show them what they were looking for. She also gave everyone a small tight-seal plastic bag.

"Be sure to put the bones into the plastic bag as you find them," she instructed. "Some are very tiny. You may not find a complete skeleton, but you may find most of one. When you've gotten all the bones out of your pellet, start looking for where each one fits on the skeleton diagram. Then glue them down as you identify where they belong."

The dark brown oval pellets were about three inches long and an inch thick and felt soft and squishy.

As Michael began picking his apart, it seemed like a small treasure hunt. The first white bone he plucked out was tiny. He figured out from the diagram that this was a vertebra, one of the backbones that made up the spine.

When he looked up, he noticed Pat Jenkins was looking at him. She quickly looked down at her work. Pat was the nosiest girl he knew, and she talked to him a lot. Michael didn't mind because she always knew the latest news about what was going on. He joked that he thought Pat had radar ears because she often overheard what he and his friends were talking about and came over to join in. He glanced up and saw Pat just turning her head away from his direction. Had she been looking at him again?

"Oh!" exclaimed Kim Offenberg from across the

9

room. "Here's a skull! It still has teeth in it!" Everybody crowded around to look. The skull was about an inch long with two extra-long teeth like fangs in the upper jaw. Michael thought that if it hadn't been so small, it would have been pretty scary looking. Kim compared it to the diagrams and identified it as a shrew.

Several more people found skulls. Michael found lots of bones but no skull. He started matching and gluing them to the diagram.

When it was time to move on to math, Mrs. Black told them to put their materials into their plastic bags to work on again tomorrow.

At recess the playground had been cleared of glass. Michael and his friends, Chad Palmer and Brad Chan, usually played ball, but today they walked around looking at the spray-painted graffiti and talking about what jerks the vandals were.

Chad remarked, "At least they didn't break any windows."

"The glass looked like it was from bottles," said Brad.

Amid the usual shrieking and shouting, Michael noticed Kim Offenberg and Pat Jenkins walking toward them. Sometimes girls would come over in bunches of twos or threes and one would tell a boy she liked him.

This hardly ever happened to Michael. When it did, he felt flattered—unless it was someone he didn't want to like him that way. No matter who it was, he never knew what to say.

Kim and Pat were almost up to them. Kim was looking at the ground. Pat Jenkins was looking right at Michael. Oh, no. He didn't want Pat Jenkins to like him. But then Kim said to Chad, "I like you."

"Oh," said Chad. He smiled and looked down as if he had taken a sudden interest in his shoelaces. Michael was glad to see that Chad didn't know what to say, either. The girls hurried away to the other side of the playground. They started talking to three other girls. They all kept sneaking looks over at the boys as if they were talking about them.

Michael elbowed Chad in the ribs. "She likes you," he said, chuckling. Chad just grinned.

Brad said, "A couple of weeks ago, she liked Matt Moore."

"Yeah," said Chad. "Every couple of weeks they decide they like somebody else." But he looked very pleased about Kim liking him now.

Brad elbowed Michael. "I think Pat Jenkins likes you," he teased. "She's always talking to you."

Michael poked him playfully in the ribs. Brad poked him back, and they started to tussle. A whistle blew. The teacher on playground duty pointed at them and shook her head.

Chapter 3

When Michael got home from school, he took off his socks, sealed them up with the leftover one in the plastic bag, and put on another pair. He wore two pairs of socks a day because Stanley usually ate four dirty ones each night.

They set out for the greenhouse with the boys holding on to the plants' main stalks to push them along. People taking giant plants for a walk on skateboards was an unusual sight. People in cars and kids on bicycles slowed to look.

After they had walked about half a mile on Oak Street, the sidewalk began slanting upward. Pushing the plants was harder. Norman let go of Fluffy for a moment to stop and scratch his nose. Fluffy started rolling backward.

Mom warned, "Don't let him get away from you. We don't want any more wild chases."

"They didn't mean to roll away those times," Michael reminded her. "It just accidentally happened."

"Don't take chances," said Mom. "The neighbors are still talking about the morning we all had to chase after Fluffy for blocks in our pajamas."

Near the top of the hill, a large greenhouse building came into view. The sign said: McDougall Plants. Mom held the door open while Michael and Norman rolled Stanley and Fluffy through. The glass-paned roof and walls flooded the place with sunlight. As far as they could see, there was greenery. Some plants in bloom made bright spots of white, yellow, red, pink, and purple. The warm air smelled of damp earth. The place was silent, except for the sound of water slowly dripping.

Mom called out, "Hello! Anybody here?"

"Coming!" answered a far-off man's voice. "I'll be there in a minute!"

From one of the aisles between the greenery rolled a gray-haired man in a wheelchair. He was running it by controls on one of its arms. On his lap sat a tray full of small plants.

Mom said, "I called about having our plants repotted. Are you John McDougall?"

"Yes," he said, taking a good look at Fluffy and Stanley. "I see why you didn't want to do it yourselves." He inspected them carefully. "Just checking," he said, "for insects or diseases. I don't want to let any of those in.

"I'm really interested to see these plants," he said. "I read an article about this species in a botany magazine—and about how the researcher was training them to do simple tasks. It was fascinating that they were

13

known only as fossils and thought to be extinct for millions of years. Isn't it amazing that once in a while an exciting discovery like that happens?''

Mom said, ''That article was by our friend Dr. Susan Sparks. She's the one doing the research.''

''She's a botanist,'' said Norman. ''That means plant scientist.''

Mr. McDougall smiled. ''I know,'' he said. ''Did you get these from Dr. Sparks?''

''She got hers from us,'' said Norman proudly. ''We gave her some seeds and some baby plants that grew from our seeds.''

''Then where did you get yours?''

Mom explained, ''My son Michael likes to send away for things—like mail in twelve proofs of purchase and a couple of dollars. One day in the mail he got two seeds. The leaflet called them 'Amazing Beans.' But he didn't remember what deal they were from, and he lost the instruction leaflet. So we had no idea what we were getting into when the boys started growing these.''

Mr. McDougall asked, ''What tasks have they been trained to do?''

''They pick things up,'' said Michael, leaving out the part about eating socks. Mom put a finger to her lips to signal Norman not to blab about other weird things the plants could do.

Norman, without thinking, blurted out, ''And the Hokey Pokey.''

Mr. McDougall burst out laughing. ''You have a great sense of humor,'' he told Norman. ''And an even better imagination. Training a plant to do the Hokey Pokey! That's a good one! Can you picture that?''

14

"Yes," said Mom. She quickly changed the subject. "Now, about repotting our plants. I have a list here of what Susan Sparks said they need in their soil mixture."

"Follow me," said Mr. McDougall. He led them to stacks of pots and other containers and selected the size that Stanley and Fluffy needed.

"Is plastic all right?" he asked. "They're lighter than clay pots and don't break easily."

"Fine," said Mom. "Norman's starting karate lessons, so we may have to replace everything in the house with things that don't break." She smiled at Norman and smoothed his hair with her hand. He grinned back.

Michael said, "Plastic lamps. Plastic beds. Plastic tables. Plastic couch." Norman elbowed him in the back.

"That's enough," ordered Mom. They pushed the plants on to the potting area.

Norman kept staring at the wheelchair. He looked at Mr. McDougall with a very concerned expression.

"Did you hurt your legs?" he asked.

Mom put her hand on Norman's shoulder. "Honey," she said, "it's not polite to ask questions like that."

"That's all right," said Mr. McDougall. "I don't mind. My legs were hurt in a very bad accident. A drunk driver ran into my car. I had to have some operations. Getting better has taken a long time. I use crutches now when I'm not at work. But I still use the wheelchair here to get around fast. It's a big place."

"I'm glad you're getting better," said Mom.

"Me, too," said Norman.

While Mr. McDougall mixed the soil, Michael, Norman, and Mom started taking off the wrappings of wires that fastened the plants' pots to the skateboards.

15

Mr. McDougall started with Stanley, who towered above him because he was sitting down.

"Will you boys give me a hand with this?" he asked. "My helpers are all out on errands."

"Okay," said Michael. "What are we supposed to do?"

"Let's do it the easy way. Instead of trying to lift the plant up, tip it over and lay it down on the floor. One of you pull this way, low on the main stem. The other one pull the other way on the pot."

The boys tipped Stanley over gently and got the pot off. Mr. McDougall put some new soil in the bottom of the larger pot. Michael slid the pot on over Stanley's roots. They raised the plant upright. Mr. McDougall poured soil into the space left in the new pot, pressed it down, and added some water. Mom and Michael hoisted Stanley up on his skateboard and started wrapping the wires around to secure him.

Norman spotted a nearby desk chair with wheels on its legs. He sat on it and pushed it around with his feet.

"Whee! It's a wheelchair!" he said.

"Get off," commanded Mom.

"That's okay," said Mr. McDougall. "Kids like to play with that chair. When we get done, will you boys show me how your plants pick things up?"

Michael replied. "They mostly do it late at night. In the daytime, they usually just stand around doing nothing like regular plants."

Mr. McDougall laughed as he mixed more soil for Fluffy.

"Plants are hardly ever doing nothing," he said. "They grow, reach out, sprout new leaves, and drop old

16

ones. They turn toward the light and get pollinated. To spread their seeds, they drop them or throw them. Some seeds fly on the breeze or float away on water. Some hitch a ride with animals. Plants are always busy.''

Michael said, ''We saw speeded-up videos of plants in school. They wiggled and waved and grew and burst buds open. But they do it too slowly for us to see.''

Norman said, ''The Venus'-flytrap is fast. When a bug lands, WHAP!'' He slapped his hands together. ''You can see that!''

''I've got a few of those in back,'' said Mr. McDougall.

Norman raised his eyebrows and rolled his eyes.

''No more plants,'' said Mom.

''I didn't say anything,'' said Norman.

''I saw what you were thinking,'' she said.

After Stanley was fastened to his skateboard, Michael parked his plant near the counter to get him out of the way. They went to work on repotting Fluffy.

When Mom and Norman were reattaching Fluffy to his skateboard, Michael said, ''Can I go look around?''

''Sure,'' said Mr. McDougall. ''For the Venus'-flytraps, go ten aisles down and turn left, then right at the next cross aisle.''

Mom said, ''Don't touch anything.''

''I want to look, too,'' said Norman.

''When we get finished with Fluffy,'' said Mom.

Michael kept stopping to look at interesting plants. As he wandered deeper into the greenhouse, he lost count of the aisles. And was he supposed to turn right and then left? Or left and then right? He didn't find the flytraps, but he did find something else very interesting.

17

Several large groups of plants had signs in front of them that said: RESERVED FOR RARE PLANT AUCTION. Michael tried to read the handprinted labels that told what kinds they were. They were all botanical names in Latin that he would have trouble pronouncing.

He heard voices coming his way. Norman was babbling about how great the flytraps were. His brother appeared around a corner with Mom and Mr. McDougall.

"We wondered where you were," said Mom.

Mr. McDougall said, "Here are some of the wonderful donations we've received for the auction so far. More are coming."

Mom said, "Our neighbor Barbara Smith is one of the chairmen. She's president of the African Violet Club."

"I know her well," said Mr. McDougall. "Has she sold you tickets yet?"

"No, but we wouldn't be interested in buying any plants anyway. How much do some of these cost?" asked Mom. "I'm just curious."

"These here might go at about fifty dollars each. And this one probably three hundred. Some even more." He pointed out several others.

Mom glanced at her watch. "It's later than I thought," she remarked. "We'll come back and look around some other time."

Mr. McDougall led them back to the front of the building. Mom went with him to the counter to pay. Fluffy was waiting where Norman had left him. But Stanley was gone.

Chapter 4

Michael asked Norman, "Did you move Stanley?"

"No, he was right here next to Fluffy. Uh-oh."

"Uh-oh is right," agreed Michael. "You go that way. I'll go this way. Run!" They took off in opposite directions.

"Boys," called Mom from the counter. "Let's go!" When she got no reply, she came to where Fluffy stood alone. No Michael. No Norman. And no Stanley. She heard the boys far off calling, "Stanley! Stanley!"

"Uh-oh," said Mom.

Mr. McDougall asked, "Is something wrong?"

She replied, "The boys seem to have taken one of their plants way back into the greenhouse. I'm not sure why." She called, "Michael! Norman!" They did not answer.

Mr. McDougall said, "You go that way, and I'll go this way. Yell if you find them first." He zoomed away, calling, "Boys! Your mother's ready to leave."

"Norman! Michael!" called Mom. For good measure, she also called, "Stanley!"

Both boys had not answered yet because they expected to find Stanley around every corner. They ran into each other where two aisles crossed.

"We're coming," yelled Michael. "We'll be there in a minute!" He whispered to Norman, "Go find Mom and stall her as long as you can. I'll keep looking."

But Mr. McDougall suddenly rolled around the corner. "Here they are!" he called to Mom. "Where did you leave your plant?" he asked the boys.

"He got lost," replied Norman.

Mom called, "Here's Stanley! By the auction plants!"

Mr. McDougall led the boys there. "How did it get here?" he asked.

Michael explained, "He uses his vines to grab on to things and pull himself around on his skateboard. But mostly only at home at night."

Mr. McDougall looked impressed. "How did you train it to do that?"

"I didn't. Both our plants started doing it on their own," replied Michael.

"That's amazing!" said Mr. McDougall. "That wasn't in the article I read."

Mom explained, "Susan Sparks was just writing about the ones she's experimenting with."

Mr. McDougall said with a smile, "I'm glad I don't have a whole greenhouse full of plants like yours. My customers would have to chase them down before they could buy them."

Norman suggested helpfully, "You could give them lassos to catch the plants."

"Come on," said Mom. "We have to get going."

Norman continued, "And cowboy hats."

Mom said, "He's a very creative thinker."

Seeing a large, graceful plant growing over a trellis, Mom asked, "What's this?"

"An old-fashioned climbing rose," said Mr. McDougall. "It's not for sale, although we do root cuttings to sell. As you can see, it's planted in the ground. It's lived here for more than fifty years. My father planted it when he ran the business. It's like an old friend."

"I didn't know greenhouses had plants that live there all the time," said Mom.

"Many do. As a matter of fact, there's going to be one of those in the auction. It's being donated by a grower who's closing because he's sold his property for a housing development. He needs to find a new home for a fifty-year-old cactus. It'd be too stressful for the plant to dig it up and move it around a lot, so we'll just show a videotape of it at the auction. And we're contacting people who might have room for something that big. It's fourteen feet tall."

Norman looked curiously at the climbing rose. "Where are the rose flowers?" he asked.

"It's not in bloom right now," explained Mr. McDougall.

As Norman turned away, one of his shoelaces came untied. He tripped on it and fell against the rose.

"Ow!" he exclaimed.

"Be careful of the thorns," said Mr. McDougall.

"My shirt's caught."

21

"Hold still so I can get you unhooked."

Norman grabbed at a branch to pull it off his sleeve, but thorns stabbed his fingers. "Ow! Make it let go!"

"Don't pull," warned Mr. McDougall. "It'll rip your shirt." He gently unhooked Norman from the sharp thorns that clawed him. Norman put his bleeding fingers in his mouth.

"Thorns really hurt," he complained.

Mr. McDougall said, "I've got a first aid kit in the office. We'll fix you right up."

"How come roses have thorns?" asked Norman.

Mr. McDougall replied, "Lots of plants have thorns. Have you ever picked blackberries? Thorns are like a self-defense system."

"Like karate?" asked Norman.

"Not exactly."

Michael pointed to some cactuses bristling with sharp spines. "Those look like self-defense plants, too," he said.

"Right," agreed Mr. McDougall. "Getting stuck with cactus spines can be painful. Animals don't want to munch on plants that will hurt them. So they leave them alone."

He added, "I have what I call security plants growing outside the back door to discourage break-ins—thorny bushes and stinging nettles. Don't ever touch stinging nettles."

"You should get some poison ivy, too," suggested Michael.

"Good idea," said Mr. McDougall, "but it takes a long time to start itching. Nettles sting right away."

When Michael started pushing Stanley along, he did

not get far because the plant was holding on to a water pipe to keep from being moved. Michael unwound Stanley's vine from the pipe and, pushing on, followed Mr. McDougall to the front of the building. When they got there, Michael was glad to see that Fluffy had not wandered off.

Mr. McDougall disinfected Norman's scratches and stabs and stuck little bandages on his fingers. "You're almost as good as new," he said.

He handed Mom a flyer about the benefit auction from a stack on the counter. "In case you change your mind," he said.

On the way home, Norman said, "I wonder why Stanley was running around in the greenhouse."

Michael replied, "I think he liked it there. He and Fluffy have never been in a place with so many other plants before. Maybe he was trying to make friends."

"I hope not," said Mom. "That's all we need—for him to invite a bunch of plants over to visit."

"That'd be cool," said Norman. "They could have a pizza party."

"I'm joking," said Mom.

"Me, too," said Norman.

Michael remarked, "Stanley and Fluffy would rather have a sock party."

Now they were walking downhill, so the plants rolled very easily. The boys had to hang on hard to keep them from going too fast.

Chapter 5

After dinner Mrs. Smith came over to sell them tickets for the fund-raiser.

Mom explained, "We wouldn't buy any plants, so there's no point in our going. Maybe we could just make a donation instead. Gardens for children are certainly a good cause."

Mrs. Smith replied, "Not everyone wants to buy at the auction, but it'll be fun to watch. And it's only part of the event. There'll be a delicious dinner—and so many interesting people—and plants you'd probably never see otherwise."

Dad asked, "Is this something we could take the whole family to?"

"Oh, yes," said Mrs. Smith. "I think the boys will enjoy it."

Dad asked Mom, "Do you want to go?"

"As long as we don't have to buy any plants," she replied. He wrote a check for four tickets.

Mrs. Smith thanked him. "Our children's project is going to be wonderful," she said. "We're also going to have a summer vegetable-growing project and work with the schools. And if we raise enough money, we'll have a Plantmobile—a van to deliver supplies to the gardens and visit schools with learning materials."

Norman asked, "Is the Plantmobile going to be green?"

"Of course," replied Mrs. Smith. "Isn't that the only color a Plantmobile should be?"

Norman told her his latest news. "I'm taking karate," he said. "Starting tomorrow. Bob is too."

"I bet you'll be good at it," she said. "And Bob, too." Mrs. Smith got up to leave. "One other thing," she added. "We're asking some people who have unusual plants to bring them to display that evening—as an extra attraction. Can we use yours?"

Norman said, "Fluffy would like to go to a party."

Dad shook his head. "Taking them anywhere is difficult and always leads to problems."

"Don't worry about that," Mrs. Smith said. "A truck rental company is donating its services. It'll carry the plants free of charge from the greenhouse to the hotel where the party will be. They can stop here to pick yours up. Besides, there weren't any problems when I borrowed them for decoration at my son's wedding."

Michael recalled that Mrs. Smith and Mom and Dad had not seen Stanley reach out and catch the bride's bouquet when she threw it to her friends. They also had not seen both plants dancing wildly next to the dessert table when the band started playing the Hokey Pokey.

The boys had gotten the plants under control without a dessert disaster, but it was a close call.

"We'll have to think about it," Mom told Mrs. Smith.

"Oh, come on, say yes," urged Mrs. Smith. "It's for a very good cause."

It was hard to say no to her because she was such a good friend.

Dad asked Mom, "What do you think?" She shrugged her shoulders. Michael thought if the plants started doing anything weird at the party, he and Norman would be there to stop them.

"Well, okay," decided Dad.

At bedtime, the boys put out the plants' sock dinners as usual.

Mom came in and said to Michael, "Hand it over."

"What?"

"Your flashlight. No reading after lights out. You're not getting enough sleep."

"But I need my flashlight. What if we have a power failure?"

"Then I'll give it back to you," she said.

After the boys were tucked in and the lights turned out, Michael waited until he heard the TV turned on low in the living room, where Mom and Dad had gone.

He whispered to Norman, "Let me use your flashlight."

"What'll you give me?"

"A baseball card."

"Two," demanded Norman.

"Deal," agreed Michael. He would give him a couple he didn't want anyway.

As he switched on the flashlight to read under the covers, he said, "I still wonder if Stanley was trying to make friends at the greenhouse."

Norman replied, "He doesn't need other plant friends. He's got Fluffy."

"But they grew up together," said Michael. "They're more like brothers."

"I don't think they're brothers," said Norman. "They never fight."

Late that night, long after the whole family had gone to sleep, the plants began to stir, ready for their nightly meal. Stanley reached out a vine and curled its tip around one of the dirty socks on the floor. He lifted it to one of the ice-cream-cone-shaped leaves that he used for eating. Slowly he sucked it in. *Schlurrrp!* After a while, he burped and reached for another one.

Fluffy did the same with the clean socks Norman had put out. Tonight they were having Fluffy's favorite sock flavor, white with brown stripes, which the boys called fudge ripple. Each of Fluffy's burps was followed by an odd noise that sounded like "Ex" because Norman had tried to teach his plant to say "Excuse me."

After dinner, Stanley and Fluffy were ready to play. Using their vines to grab on to furniture, they pulled themselves out of the boys' room and down the hall toward the living room. Tonight they headed straight for the closet by the front door to get their favorite toys—the remote control trucks the boys' grandmother had given them for Christmas.

Twisting and tugging the doorknob, Stanley got the closet open. He grabbed the control for one truck with a vine, turned it on, and started working it. After running the truck into the wall a couple of times, he got it to run out of the closet and grabbed on to it with another vine.

With the truck towing him, off Stanley went—from the living room, through the dining room, into the kitchen, out into the hall, and back into the living room again. Fluffy followed with the other truck. Around and around in the house they went, trying to race each other.

When they got tired of that, they ran the trucks back into the closet. Stanley searched around with a vine until he found the TV remote control. He turned on the TV and kept changing channels but couldn't seem to find anything he liked. He turned the TV off and dropped the remote on the coffee table in front of the couch. Stanley and Fluffy pulled themselves back to the boys' room and settled in their usual places.

Chapter 6

Late the next afternoon, Norman came back from his first karate lesson all excited. Dad got home at the same time.

"How did your lesson go?" Dad asked.

"Fine," replied Norman.

"What exactly did you learn?"

"We learned to stretch to warm up and bow and pay attention and not horse around."

Dad smiled. "That sounds like a good start," he remarked.

"This is how we bow," Norman said. Pressing his arms to his sides, he bent at the waist.

"Very good," said Dad. "Keep up the good work. And be careful not to hit the furniture."

"We didn't start the hitting part yet," explained Norman. "Or the kicking part either."

Norman followed Dad into the kitchen, bowed to Mom, and said "Arigato, sensay."

"Huh?" said Mom.

Norman bragged, "I'm talking Japanese."

"What did you say?" she asked.

"Arigato means thank you. Sensay means teacher. That's what we say to our teacher. Arigato, sensay."

At dinner, Norman said "Arigato" every time food was passed to him. Michael got tired of Norman showing off and started saying "Gracias."*

Norman frowned. "You're supposed to say arigato," he said.

Michael looked down his nose at his brother. "Gracias is thank you in Spanish. Everybody knows that." They kept up with arigato and gracias, just to irritate each other.

When Dad handed Mom the green beans, she winked at him and said, "Merci."†

"What's that?" asked Norman.

"Thank you in French," she replied. She handed the salad to Dad.

"Danke,"‡ he said. "That's thank you in German."

For the rest of the meal, the thank-yous in four languages were flying around the table. Finally, when Mom passed Norman his dessert, he responded, "Arigato, gracias, merci, danke."

"You're very, very, very, very polite," she said.

Norman stood up and took a bow.

After dinner, Mom answered the kitchen phone. "Susan!" she said. "How are you? What's new?"

*Pronounced *gra-see-ahs.*
†Pronounced *mare-see.*
‡Pronounced *dahn-kah.*

Mom and Dr. Sparks always talked for a long time. When Mom got off the phone, she came in the living room with news.

"Susan's driving to Elmville to help with plants for the rain forest exhibit. She said the zoo's letting some people into the rain forest for previews. If we want to go, she can get us in, so I invited them to spend the night with us. It's not far out of their way to come here first."

"It'll be good to see them," said Dad. "Is the whole family coming?"

"Just Susan and the kids. Fred has to work."

Norman was delighted that his friend Max was coming. Max was a year younger and liked to join in whatever Norman did. Michael was not sure how he felt about Sarah coming to visit. She was his age, knew more about plants than he did, and kept letting him know it.

Mom continued, "We'll put Susan and Sarah in the boys' room. Max can sleep on the couch and you two can use your sleeping bags on the living room floor."

"Why do they have to sleep in *our* room?" complained Michael. "I don't want a girl sleeping in there with all my stuff."

Mom replied, "All your stuff is put away since you promised to be neat in return for keeping your plant."

"But what if she looks in my dresser drawers?" persisted Michael.

"She's not going to do that."

"But how do you know? She might when nobody's looking."

"Yeah," added Norman. "When I slept over at Bob's

one time, when nobody was looking, I looked in his dresser drawers.''

Mom scolded, ''You shouldn't have done that!''

Michael added, ''He snoops everywhere in this house.''

''Do not!'' protested Norman. Then he thought for a moment. ''What if Sarah looks in my underwear drawer?''

Mom assured him, ''She has a brother, so she's seen boys' underwear before. She won't be interested in looking at yours.''

Dad laughed. ''Why don't you just tape all your dresser drawers shut? Then you won't have to worry.''

Mom said, ''I think Susan and Sarah would find that extremely weird.''

Norman said cheerfully, ''I'll only tape my underwear drawer.''

Michael said, ''We'll take the plants in the living room with us.''

''Fine,'' said Mom. ''We don't want them wandering down the hall in the middle of the night looking for you. But Susan'll probably set an alarm so she can get up and watch them eat and anything else they do. She did that when we stayed at their house.''

Norman usually watered Fluffy with his Super Splasher Water Blaster. This irritated Michael because Norman's aim was not always on target. Sometimes he missed and watered the rug or Michael by mistake. At least, he said it was a mistake. Once in a while, Fluffy got hold of the Blaster and tried to water himself. Fluffy's aim was worse than Norman's. This would not have been a big problem if Norman didn't occasionally load the Blaster with something other than water. Once he and Bob had filled it with liquid soap and grape juice to make purple slime. Expecting water, Fluffy had accidentally slimed himself and most of the kitchen.

Michael usually watered Stanley with a big pitcher. Once in a while, when he had a lot on his mind, he forgot.

One afternoon, when he had taken Stanley out in the backyard for some sun, the plant tapped him on the shoulder with a vine.

"What?" asked Michael.

Stanley pointed to his pot.

"There's nothing wrong with your pot," said Michael. "It's new."

Stanley grabbed his wrist and yanked his hand down to press it against the dirt in the pot. It felt bone-dry.

"Oh," said Michael, "I forgot." The hose was handier than going in the house to get the pitcher. "You haven't had a bath in a long time," he told Stanley. He twisted the hose nozzle to get a fine spray.

The plant shivered a little when the cold water pattered on his leaves.

Michael remarked, "This is sort of like being in a rain forest, but the rain there is probably a lot warmer."

Stanley rubbed some vines up and down on other vines, like a person washing in the shower. Michael also aimed some water into the pot. He was careful not to flood it because too much water is not good for most plants. When Michael shut off the hose, Stanley was dripping all over.

Mom opened the back door. "Don't try to bring that

wet plant in the house," she said. "Either get some towels and wipe off every leaf and vine—or stay out there with him until he dries."

Stanley decided to do something else. He shook himself like a huge wet dog. Drops of water whirled everywhere. Mom ducked inside the door in time, but Michael got completely splattered. Mom brought him a towel.

"Stanley would make a good lawn sprinkler," she said, laughing. "Maybe you could get him a part-time job."

On his way to and from Bob's house, Norman often stopped to talk to Mrs. Smith when she was out working in her yard. She thought anything he did was wonderful. Her little brown dog, Margo, was also always glad to see him.

"Want to hear a funny joke?" he asked her.

"Okay," said Mrs. Smith.

"Why do plants like football and baseball and basketball and soccer and hockey games?"

Mrs. Smith replied, "I don't know. Why do they?"

"They like to root for their teams. Get it? Plants root!"

"That's a good one," she said, laughing.

"A kid in my karate class told it to me."

"How's your class going?"

"I like it. Some of it's hard to do, but it's fun. This is how we bow," Norman said, bowing. "And we talk Japanese. We say 'Arigato, sensay,' to our teacher. That means 'Thank you, teacher.' "

"You're speaking Japanese!" exclaimed Mrs. Smith. "That's wonderful."

"Yeah," agreed Norman.

She asked, "When you get good at karate, you're not going to use it to attack anybody, are you?"

"No, the sensay says we're not allowed to use it for attacking—only for defending ourselves and our loved ones. You're my friend, so after I get good at karate, if you need defending, let me know."

"I'll do that," said Mrs. Smith.

Norman came home from each karate lesson very excited about what he and Bob were learning. Some afternoons they practiced together. Mom shooed them out of the living room because she said they were making the lamps an endangered species. So they went through the motions in the basement.

Norman often practiced on his own in the boys' room early in the morning. First he stretched to warm up. Then he repeated the basic moves for a few minutes.

Dad ordered him not to yell "Hi! Ah!" when others were still asleep. So Norman said it quietly.

He began trying to teach his plant what he had learned. He lifted one of Fluffy's vines and moved it back and forth in a punching motion, over and over. But when he let go of the vine, Fluffy let it fall limply.

Norman kept trying with one vine after another, hoping Fluffy would get interested and do it on his own. But he didn't. Norman remembered that it had taken endless repetitions to teach both plants how to catch and toss and do the Hokey Pokey. He decided not to give up.

Chapter 7

To get ready for their visitors, Mom organized the chores. She baked goodies and mopped the kitchen floor. Norman dusted. Michael ran the vacuum. Dad put clean sheets on the boys' beds. The boys moved their plants into the living room. Norman got a roll of masking tape from the basement and taped his underwear drawer shut.

"Norman, that's ridiculous," said Mom. "What are Susan and Sarah going to think when they see that?"

"I don't care," said Norman.

Michael didn't say anything, but he wished he had thought of it first. Because it was Norman's idea, he couldn't do it, too. So he emptied his underwear drawer into a cardboard box he got from the basement. He hid the box behind the living room couch, near where he would put his sleeping bag.

*   *   *

When the Sparkses' van pulled into the drive, the whole family went out to greet them. Susan Sparks hugged Mom and Dad. Norman and Max jumped up and down to show how glad they were to see each other. Norman bowed to Dr. Sparks.

"He's learning karate," explained Dad.

Michael said "Hi" to Sarah.

"Hi," she replied.

Michael noticed four large plants in the back of the van.

"What are these for?" he asked.

"They're from the research center where my mom works," Sarah explained. "We're delivering them to the rain forest exhibit."

Dr. Sparks said, "They're tropical plants, so we have to bring them in the house for the night to keep them warm. Besides, they're very rare. I wouldn't risk leaving them in the van."

"I wouldn't either," agreed Dad. "There's been some vandalism in the area lately."

Mom said, "We can put them in the dining room."

Although the visiting plants were not more than three feet tall, with their large clay pots they were heavy. Dr. Sparks had brought a low wooden platform with wheels and a rope handle to move them easily, one by one.

Michael helped bring them in. Each was a different kind. One was a beautiful fern with feathery fronds.

"Ferns don't have seeds," Sarah said.

"I know," said Michael. "They reproduce by spores that grow on the undersides of their fronds and fall on the ground."

"Are you still reading books about plants?" she said.

37

"Yeah, I read all the time." He did not mention that most of the books he had been reading lately were like *The Curse of the Evil Ooze* and *The Ghost of Creep Castle.*

Sarah bragged, "I read plant books all the time, too. Did you know there are seven hundred and fifty-eight species of ferns?"

"Really?" asked Michael.

"No," answered Sarah. "I just made that up. It was a trick question. If you said you knew that, that'd prove you were faking like Max does. He's always pretending he knows when he really doesn't. He's such a pest sometimes."

Michael asked, "How's your night-blooming cereus that we saw when we stayed at your house?"

"It's not blooming this time of year," she replied, "but it's fine. I got a new African violet—a rare one with yellow flowers."

Michael said, "Our neighbor, Mrs. Smith, has one of those. She's got dozens of African violets. I plant-sit for them when she goes on trips."

"Can we go see them?"

"Sure," he said.

Michael looked closely at the fourth plant. It had smooth-edged, light green leaves and short, slender vines all over that ended in pretty little curls at the tips.

"What's this one?" he asked.

"It's a kongabonga plant," said Sarah, "from the rain forests of Brazil."

Michael said, "I wonder if it ever gets homesick."

"This one never lived in a real rain forest," she explained. "It grew from seed in a greenhouse."

Dr. Sparks called the kids to come to the kitchen table.

"I brought you a little present," she told Michael and Norman. "A pizza garden."

Max said, "We have one every summer. It's fun."

Norman looked amazed. "How can that be? You invented a plant that grows pizzas?"

Sarah said, "No, it's plants that grow the things that you use to make a pizza."

Mom smiled. "I wish you *had* discovered a plant that grows pizzas. I'd love to just go out in the back yard and pick one for dinner. That would really be fast food!"

Dr. Sparks chuckled. "*That* would be a scientific breakthrough!" She took paper packets of seeds from her huge handbag. "Here's wheat," she said, "to grow the grain to make the flour to make the dough to make the crust. And here are peppers and onions. And a juicy type of Italian tomato to make sauce. And herbs—oregano, basil, parsley."

"Is there a cheese plant?" asked Norman.

"There's no such thing," said Sarah.

Michael said, "Cheese is made from milk that comes from cows that eat plants. So cheese sort of does come from plants."

"The long way around," said Mom.

Norman said, "We could grow some plants in our pizza garden for a cow to come over to eat to give us milk to make cheese for our pizza."

"No, we couldn't," said Mom.

39

Michael picked up a plastic bag labeled Peat Pellets. "What are peat pellets for?" he asked.

Mom remarked, "I hope they're not like owl pellets."

Michael suggested, "Maybe they're hawked up by a guy named Pete."

"Oh, yuck," said Norman.

"Oh, yuck," echoed Max.

Dr. Sparks explained, "These are made of dried, pressed peat moss. They're for starting your seeds indoors. They're like little magic pots."

"Magic!" exclaimed Norman. "How?"

Max said, "Wait'll you see. They're amazing!"

Dr. Sparks cut open the bag and took out a small, round, thin, dark brown disc. She handed it to Michael and then Norman. It felt dry and hard.

"Now we need a ruler, a saucer, and a glass of warm water," she said.

She instructed Michael to measure the disc. It was one and a half inches in diameter and five-eighths of an inch thick. Dr. Sparks put the disc on the saucer and gave Norman the glass of water.

"We'll time it and measure it," she said, looking at her watch. "Okay, pour enough to cover the bottom of the saucer." At first nothing happened. Then they noticed that the water was disappearing.

Michael said, "The pellet's soaking up the water. It looks like it's getting a little thicker."

Dr. Sparks announced, "One minute. Measure the thickness."

"Half an inch," reported Michael.

"More water," Dr. Sparks told Norman.

At two minutes, the pellet had swelled up to one inch

40

high. At three minutes, it had grown another half inch. At four minutes, Michael found it was one and three-fourth inches high.

"That's as big as it's going to get," said Dr. Sparks. She poured off the leftover water. Michael measured the diameter again. It was still only an inch and a half wide. He looked closely and saw that the now-squishy peat moss was held together in its little barrel shape by an almost invisible netting.

Dr. Sparks explained, "You just plant your seeds in these. After they've sprouted, you transplant the whole pot. I brought you a booklet on how to do it."

Michael asked, "If we started seeds right now, how long would it take to grow all the stuff to make a pizza?"

She replied, "Some plants take longer than others. You'd probably be ready to cook in about three or four months."

Norman said, "I'd get really hungry waiting that long for a pizza!"

Mom laughed. "I'm glad I don't have to start meals that far ahead."

Dr. Sparks agreed. "Thank goodness for farmers and grocery stores. But it's important to know where food comes from and how to grow it. Homegrown vegetables taste especially delicious. We have a family garden every summer to grow some of our food."

Mom said, "Our town's going to have a vegetable-growing project for kids. Our neighbor, Barbara Smith, is one of the leaders."

Max said proudly, "I'm good at hoeing and weeding and watering."

41

"And eating," added his mother, putting an arm around him. "Did you bring in your duffel bag?" Max and Norman went out to the van to get Max's things.

By the driveway they met Bob, who had come over to see what was going on. He had never met the Sparkses, but he had heard a lot about them from Norman.

"Can I go in and look at Dr. Sparks?" he asked Norman. "I never saw a botanist before."

"Okay," replied Norman.

Max bragged, "She's my mother."

They trooped into the kitchen, where the mothers were talking while dinner cooked.

"This is Norman's friend Bob," Mom told Dr. Sparks. "He lives down the street."

"Hello, Bob," Dr. Sparks said. "It's nice to meet you."

"Hi," said Bob.

Mom asked, "Would you like to stay for dinner, Bob?"

"Okay," he replied.

The mothers started talking again. Bob still stood there.

"Bob," said Mom, "did you want something else?"

He asked Dr. Sparks, "Can I have your autograph?"

"All right," she said. "Nobody's ever asked for my autograph before."

From his pocket, Bob pulled a folded-up page torn from a spiral notebook and a very short pencil. "I never saw a botanist before," he said.

42

"I'm glad you asked," said Dr. Sparks. She unfolded the paper and wrote:

"To Bob—I enjoyed meeting you at Norman's house. Have fun learning about science. Sincerely, Susan Sparks, botanist."

Bob said, "Thanks!"

Norman stepped forward. "Can I have your autograph, too?" he asked. Dr. Sparks signed a paper napkin for him. Then Max handed her another napkin.

"I want your autograph, too," he said.

"But I'm your mother. You see me every day."

"I still want your autograph."

She wrote:

"To Max, my dear and wonderful son. You are so special. Your father and I are always so proud of you. With love, from your mother the botanist, Susan Sparks."

She added X's and O's, which meant hugs and kisses.

Max looked at it and said, "This is lots of words, and I still can't read cursive too good yet."

"I forgot," said Dr. Sparks. She read the napkin to him. Max beamed with happiness. The boys ran into the living room to look at their autographs.

"I'm keeping this always," Max told Norman.

Bob said, "When I go home, I'm getting an autograph from *my* mother."

Norman went back in the kitchen and asked Mom, "Can I have your autograph?"

After Norman got a wonderful note from Mom, he and Bob and Max also got autographs from Dad. Then Norman and Bob taught Max how to bow and say arigato. Next Norman decided that he and Max should amaze Bob with the magic peat pots. The only room that had water and no people in it at the moment was the bathroom. He put a pellet in the sink, closed the drain, and ran in a little water.

"Now watch," he told Bob. "It's magic."

"Nothing's happening," said Bob.

"It will," said Norman. "See? The water's disappearing."

"It must be leaking out," said Bob. "You should get your sink fixed."

Norman said, "Doesn't the pellet look thicker?"

"No."

"Well it *is* thicker."

"It doesn't look like it," said Bob.

Norman ran more water into the sink. "Now see?"

"I guess it *is* getting bigger," admitted Bob. "It looks taller." He felt the pellet. "It's not magic," he said. "It's soaking up water."

In a couple of more minutes, the peat pellet had grown as big as it was going to get. Bob picked it up and pressed it in his hand.

"Cool," he said. "The water puffed it up."

"Don't squeeze it," said Norman. He grabbed at the pellet to get it from Bob and squeezed too hard. The almost invisible netting holding the peat together burst. It crumbled into the leftover water and made a gooey brown mess in the bottom of the sink.

44

"Uh-oh," said Max.

"Don't worry," said Norman. "I can clean it up." He rinsed and pushed the mess down the drain.

They heard Dad call, "Come on, everybody! Dinner's ready!"

Chapter 8

After dinner both families went over to Mrs. Smith's house to see her violet collection.

"Oh, Dr. Sparks," said Mrs. Smith, "I've heard so much about you. It's an honor to meet such a distinguished botanist."

"Call me Susan," replied Dr. Sparks. "I've heard many wonderful things about you, too."

Mrs. Smith told Dr. Sparks about the auction and children's garden project. She showed her yellow violet to Sarah, who told her about her own plants.

Sarah exclaimed over some violets that had frilly red and white striped blossoms.

"Would you like one to take home?" asked Mrs. Smith. "I have extras."

"Yes," said Sarah. "Thank you."

Mrs. Smith asked Max, "Would you like one, too?"

"Okay," replied Max.

His mother prodded him, "What do you say?"

He bowed to Mrs. Smith and said, "Arigato."

"Oh, he speaks Japanese," said Mrs. Smith, "just like Norman."

Norman boasted, "I taught him."

Mrs. Smith patted him on the shoulder. "You always amaze me," she said. "Every time I see you, I wonder, 'What next?' "

Later, back home, Dad asked Susan Sparks if she wanted an alarm clock to wake her up to watch what Stanley and Fluffy did during the night.

"Not tonight," she replied. "After a five-hour drive with two kids squabbling most of the way, I need a whole night's sleep. But I want to take some pictures of Stanley and Fluffy." She looked through her bag. "My camera's not here. I must have left it at home."

Dad offered, "You can use ours. I bought plenty of film for the zoo trip."

After Dr. Sparks took several photos of the boys' plants, Norman and Max wanted to get in the pictures, too. She let them stand behind the plants and peek out. They both made funny faces.

Mom said, "Let's get some pictures of the ones that are going to the rain forest." She gathered everyone in the dining room for group pictures with those plants. Then Dad took one of Mom with everybody.

Norman reached for the camera. "I want to take a picture, too," he said.

"Okay," said Dad. "But be careful. Look through here and make sure you see what you want to show in the picture."

Michael added, "Not like the last time. You took ones of people with no heads."

"They did too have heads," grumped Norman. "You just couldn't see them in the pictures."

Sarah said, "Max did that, too." Her little brother glared at her.

"Never mind, boys," said Dad. "When I got my first camera, I did that a few times myself. The only way to learn how to take pictures is to do it." He got Norman to stand in the right place and reminded him about how to operate the camera.

"And when you press the button," Dad warned, "don't dip the camera. That's what happened to the heads the last time."

"Okay," said Norman. He squinted through the view finder. "I can't see everybody," he said. The group squashed closer together.

"*Now* have you got us all in?" asked Mom.

As Norman nodded, he dipped the camera.

"Don't move it," warned Dad again. "You'll take a picture of everybody's feet."

Norman clutched the camera, thinking hard about not moving it. As he pressed the button, Dad yelled, "Wait!" The flash lit up the room.

Norman said, "I didn't move it."

Dad pointed out, "You had one hand over the lens. You just took a close-up of your fingers."

Dad rearranged Norman's fingers. This time the picture taking went perfectly.

"I want to take some more," said Norman.

"That's enough for now," replied Dad. He took the camera and put it on a shelf in the corner cupboard.

48

Soon it was bedtime. Mom put a sheet, blanket, and pillow on the living room couch for Max. Michael and Norman unrolled their sleeping bags on the floor. They put out the socks for the plants' dinner.

Sarah, who got to use the bathroom first, came out in her robe waving her toothbrush.

"There's something wrong with the sink," she said.

Dad checked, and found the drain was clogged. First he tried a rubber plunger to create suction to clear the sink pipe. The drain belched up a little brown stuff but stayed clogged. So Dad got a wrench and a pail and crouched under the sink to take the pipe apart. Everybody crammed into the bathroom and gathered around to watch.

"Wouldn't you know," said Mom, "that this would happen the one night we have guests?"

Dad suggested from under the sink, "Why don't you all go brush your teeth in the kitchen?" But they all wanted to watch him struggle with the pipe. When he got it apart, the backed-up water poured into the pail. He pried thick brown goo out of the pipe.

"What's this stuff?" he wondered. "And how did it get here?"

Sarah said, "It looks sort of like wet peat."

Dad inquired sternly, "Did anybody put wet peat down the sink?"

"Uh," said Norman.

"Yes?" asked Dad.

"We didn't mean to," explained Norman. "Max and I were just showing Bob the magic pot trick. The peat pot got squeezed too hard, and it popped peat all over."

Dad said, "Why on earth did you put it down the drain?"

"I was cleaning it up," said Norman. "I didn't know it'd get stuck."

"No more peat in any sinks," ordered Dad. He handed the pail to Michael. "Go dump this outside in a flower bed."

Norman, wanting to make amends, turned on the faucet. "See? It's working okay now!" he announced. The water ran freely down the drain, out the open pipe under the sink, and all over the floor and Dad.

Dr. Sparks grabbed some towels to sop up the flood. "Never a dull moment," she told Dad. "This is just like home."

The sink pipe was put back together. The water was cleaned up. Dad ordered Norman not to mess with any more peat pellets without adult supervision. Everyone brushed their teeth.

Dad called, "'Everybody hit the sack. We have to get up early."

Mom added, "We're having pancakes for breakfast."

Michael snuggled into his sleeping bag. He hoped that Norman and Max would fall asleep right away.

Their parents came in to say goodnight and turned out the lights. As soon as the two bedroom doors closed, Norman and Max began whispering.

"Shut up," said Michael. This only spurred them on. They acted like they were having their own private sleepover. They bounced on the couch. Norman put his lighted flashlight under his chin to make Max laugh. Norman turned on a lamp so he could show Max some karate moves. They tried to be quiet, but they kept saying "Hi! Yah!" louder and louder. This brought Mom running.

"Lie down and go to sleep," she ordered. "I don't want to hear another peep out of you." She turned off the lamp and left. As soon as he heard her bedroom door close, Norman turned the lamp back on. He and Max played at karate moves quietly for a while, but Norman tripped over Michael.

Michael felt too lazy to get out of his sleeping bag to move. He scrunched and wriggled like a caterpillar to get out of the way. He did not notice that he was now lying on top of Stanley's dinner.

Every time Norman and Max bowed to each other, they burst out laughing. Dr. Sparks and Mom both came hurrying down the hall to settle them again. After they left, silence lasted about thirty seconds. Norman started quietly singing and dancing the Hokey Pokey. Max started doing it, too. They took turns singing different body parts to put in and take out and got all mixed up. Then Fluffy joined in. Since he had trouble telling his right vines from his left and had several of each, he got all tangled up. Stanley started doing it, too. Max and Norman were laughing and singing louder and louder as they and the plants shook themselves all about.

Mom's voice boomed down the hall. "OKAY!" she yelled. "That's it!" She stormed into the living room with Dr. Sparks right behind her. "I don't know how your father can sleep through this uproar!" she shouted. "You'd better stop now, because if you don't, I'm going to wake him up. I don't think you want to deal with him again tonight, not after the peat-in-the-sink situa-

51

tion. He's sleeping with a towel over his pillow because his hair's still wet."

Michael protested, "I'm not doing anything. I'm minding my own business trying to sleep."

Dr. Sparks snapped at Max, "What do we have to do to get you two to settle down?"

Michael suggested, "Have you got any tranquilizer darts?"

Dad appeared in the doorway looking like he was sleepwalking. "What's all the yelling about?" he mumbled.

"The boys won't shut up and go to sleep," explained Dr. Sparks. "At least Sarah went to sleep right away."

Dad said, "Boys, shut up and go to sleep. Or no zoo trip tomorrow." He turned around and walked out.

Max made a dive landing onto the couch. He pulled the blanket up to his chin. Norman plunged feet-first deep into his sleeping bag. Not even his head was sticking out. Mom took the light bulbs out of all the lamps. She frisked Norman's sleeping bag and took away his flashlight.

Norman protested, "But I need that! What if I wake up and have to go to the bathroom?"

"The hall light's always on," Mom assured him. "Not another peep," she warned, "not a whisper, not a squeak."

Norman said, "Okay. Just burps. From Fluffy and Stanley."

Sarah appeared in the doorway. "I heard yelling. It woke me up."

Finally everyone went to sleep. Later, when the plants were ready to eat, Stanley could not find his dirty socks.

While Fluffy schlurped and burped, Stanley searched the floor with his vines. He found the cardboard box behind the couch and poked into it.

He plucked out a piece of underwear. Since it wasn't a dirty sock, he tossed it aside and reached back into the box. By the time he got to the bottom of the box, Michael's underwear was thrown all over the living room.

Chapter 9

At last Stanley sensed where his dinner was, but it was under something so big and heavy that he could not move it. He explored it until he found Michael's head sticking out. The plant tapped his nose with a vine. Michael did not stir. Stanley tickled his ear. Michael brushed the vine away without waking. Stanley wrapped the tip of a vine around a lock of Michael's hair and yanked.

"Ow!" exclaimed Michael. He grabbed the vine and untangled it from his hair. "Stanley! what are you doing?"

The plant poked him in the face with one vine and pointed to the sleeping bag with another.

There was only a very dim light from a lamp far down the hall, so Michael did not notice that the living room had been redecorated with underwear. He was staring at Stanley, and it took a while to figure out what the plant was signaling.

"Under my sleeping bag?" he said. "What's under it?"

Stanley acted out the motions of eating a sock. He pushed several vines against the sleeping bag. Michael crawled out of it and looked underneath.

"Oh," he said. "I didn't know I was sleeping on top of your food. Sorry." Stanley grabbed a dirty sock and sucked it in. *Schlurrrrrp!*

Michael moved over and went back to sleep. Stanley finished his meal.

Because the living room floor was so cluttered with Michael and Norman sleeping there, the plants did not get out the remote control trucks to run around. Instead, they pulled themselves into the dining room on the way to roam around the kitchen.

Fluffy, who was leading the way, kept going. But Stanley bumped into one of the visiting plants. He stopped to find out what it was. He poked it gently in several places. It did not touch back, but its leaves moved a little. He went on to the next visitor, and the next, touching them as if he were saying hello. When Stanley got to the kongabonga plant, one of its curly vines reached out at his touch. The tip twined around the end of his vine—like a plant handshake. Stanley rustled his leaves and burped. The kongabonga was so startled that it pressed itself back against the wall.

Exploring the dining room, Stanley found the camera. He wrapped a vine around it and shook it as he pulled himself into the kitchen. Tightening the vine around the camera, he happened to press the button. *Whirr* went the camera with a flash of bright light. He seemed startled. But evidently he enjoyed either the whirring sound

55

or the light—or both. He pressed the button over and over—whirr, flash, whirr, flash—until all the film was used up. He kept pressing the button, but nothing happened. He lost interest and dropped the camera on the kitchen table.

Even though Norman had been up late the night before, he was the first one awake in the morning as usual. He was surprised to see underwear scattered all over the living room. And he was glad to see it wasn't his. Being a natural neatness nut, he picked it up. He couldn't put it back in their room while Dr. Sparks and Sarah were in there. So he hid it under the couch cushions, although Max was still asleep on top of them.

With three extra people, there was a traffic jam waiting to use the bathroom and take showers. Mom insisted that the guests go first. Dad turned on the TV to get the weather report on the news and woke up Michael. The last one to get up, Michael went to the boys' room to get the clothes he was going to wear. Sarah was there, already dressed and tying her sneakers. She pointed to the tape on Norman's drawer.

"What's in there?" she asked.

"Norman's stuff," he said.

"Weird," said Sarah.

Michael got his jeans and shirt and headed back to the living room to get underwear from the box behind the couch. It was empty. He found Norman in the dining room, talking to Max and fiddling with his Water Blaster. Michael signaled Norman to come out in the hall with him. Max tagged along.

"Have you seen my underwear?" he whispered to his brother.

But Max also heard what he said. He asked loudly, "You lost your underwear?"

"Shhhh!" said Michael.

Norman whispered, "When I woke up, it was all over the living room. I picked it up and stuffed it under the couch cushions so nobody would see it. You should've taped your dresser drawer shut like me."

Michael went back to the living room. Sarah was there watching TV and sitting on the couch.

"Hi," said Sarah.

"Hi," he replied. He flung himself into a chair to wait for her to get up and go away. He pretended to be interested in the program. Some lady was showing how to cook a bunch of stuff.

Sarah asked, "This is boring. Where's the remote?"

He looked around. "It must be here somewhere." But he didn't find it.

Sarah stood up. "When ours gets lost, it's usually stuck between the couch cushions." Michael couldn't think of anything to say fast enough to stop her. She lifted up a cushion and saw a pile of underwear.

"What's this doing here?" she asked.

"It's Norman's," Michael lied out of embarrassment. "He keeps his clothes in funny places."

"He's *very* weird," said Sarah. She put the cushion back.

Mom called, "Come to breakfast, everybody!"

Sarah went into the dining room. Michael grabbed his underwear along with his other clothes and ran for the bathroom. He took a ten-second shower and quickly got dressed. Seeing in the mirror that his hair was going every which way, he carefully combed it down. He tied his shoes. He tucked his shirt in evenly all the way around.

At the dining room table, he sat in the only chair left, next to Sarah.

Mom came from the kitchen carrying a platter heaped with pancakes. She noticed the new and improved son who had made himself look good without being nagged.

"Michael!" she said. "You look . . ."

Oh, no, he thought. *She's going to tell everybody I combed my hair.* He wanted to crawl under the table from embarrassment. He saw Dad catch her eye and shake his head slightly.

"Hungry," Mom said. "You look really hungry this morning." She passed him the pancakes.

"Gracias," said Michael. He forked three onto his plate and passed the platter to Sarah.

"Arigato," she said, grinning.

"Hey," complained Max. "Only Norman and Bob and me are supposed to say that."

Sarah replied, "Anybody can say anything they want! Arigato, arigato, arigato!"

Dr. Sparks shook her head. "Just like home," she said.

"Yes," agreed Mom.

"Is there any more syrup?" asked Dad, holding up a nearly empty bottle.

"Where's the other big bottle?" asked Mom. "I put two on the table."

Norman and Max put their heads together and giggled as if they knew something nobody else was in on. Norman slid off his chair. He opened the bottom doors of the corner cupboard and took out his Blaster. In the cupboard could be seen a large syrup bottle. It was empty.

"Oh, no," said Mom.

Norman aimed the Blaster at the pancake on Max's plate and squirted a puddle of syrup on it. Max chuckled with delight.

"More! More!" shouted Max.

Sarah laughed and held out her plate. Michael did, too, because that was the only way he was ever going to get any syrup.

Norman went around the table, syrup-blasting on every plate. For once, his aim was perfect.

Dad told him sternly, "We'll discuss this later. At least you didn't get syrup all over yourself or anybody else."

"Anybody want some more?" offered Norman. "I got plenty left." But everyone had enough. He put the Blaster down in the middle of the table.

After pancakes, Sarah started eating a banana. "Banana plants," she said, "grow really fast. In only six months, one can get ten feet tall. And in nine months, it can get twenty or thirty feet high. That's as big as they get."

Dad commented, "Remind me not to get one of those for my office."

Norman reached for a banana in the fruit bowl.

Sarah continued, "Many species of bananas are pollinated by bats."

Norman put the banana back in the bowl.

"Bats are our friends," Sarah added, taking a big bite of her banana. "They eat tons of insects and pollinate many plants." Norman looked totally grossed out.

"Do they touch strawberries?" he asked.

"No," said Dr. Sparks. "And they don't touch the actual bananas, either. The fruit grows after pollination."

Norman helped himself to some strawberries.

Michael wanted to add some impressive plant facts to the conversation. He said, "The biggest trees are the giant sequoias and redwoods in northern California. Some are over three-hundred-and-fifty feet tall and three or four-thousand years old."

Norman laughed. "Do they get a birthday cake with four thousand candles on it? It would take a big wind to blow all those out." Max giggled.

Mom said, "Those trees make the huge two-hundred-year-old oaks in our local park seem like toddlers."

"The oldest living trees," said Sarah, "are the bristlecone pines in California. They don't get very big, but one is about four thousand seven hundred years old."

"I've seen pictures of those old ones," said Michael. "They look partly dead, but they're not."

Mom said, "Let's save the rest of the dueling plant facts for later, everybody. Finish your breakfast. We have to get going."

Chapter 10

After eating, they all quickly cleared the dirty dishes. Norman didn't have time to clean the syrup out of his Blaster so he stowed it under his bed, where he usually kept it.

The Sparkses packed up because they were going straight home from the zoo. Before Sarah zipped her duffle bag, Michael noticed two books sticking up. He peeked to see what they were—*Amazing Plant Facts* and *The Ghost of Gruesome Gulch*.

Mom rode with Dr. Sparks in her van so they could talk. Sarah went with them. The boys rode with Dad in his car. Michael took a book along so he wouldn't have to listen to Norman and Max being silly in the back seat. Dad turned his favorite music station on loud so he wouldn't have to listen, either.

No matter how hard he concentrated on his book, Michael could not help hearing Norman telling Max dumb jokes. Max laughed like crazy. Once or twice Michael had to laugh in spite of himself. He looked over at Dad and saw he was chuckling, too.

After an hour and a half, they pulled into the parking lot at the Elmville Zoo. In front of a large building was a sign: RAIN FOREST EXHIBIT—OPENING SOON.

Mom and Sarah were waiting for them by the door.

"Susan said she'll be in the zoo greenhouses for at least a couple of hours," said Mom. "She'll catch up with us later."

Inside they found a woman in a tan zoo uniform. They told her Dr. Sparks had arranged their visit. "Welcome," she said. "I hope you'll enjoy your preview. At the end, we'd like you to fill out questionnaires about the rain forest experience. The waterfall's not turned on today, and the gift shop and snack bar aren't open yet. But almost everything else is ready for visitors. And the rest rooms are to the left."

"It feels like summer in here," said Norman.

"It's kept at eighty degrees with lots of humidity," said the woman.

High up on the stone wall where the waterfall would come down, a mist sprayed out. Dad led the way into what looked like a small forest inside a very high glass roof and walls. It was packed with trees and shorter plants. A few empty spaces were left for more to be added. Following a paved path, they stopped to look at especially interesting ones and read the labels.

Bamboo grew high above their heads. A sign explained that mahogany and kapok trees can grow to two hundred feet tall, and that only the highest trees get full sunlight. Plants on the forest floor grow in their shade.

When Sarah pointed out a six-foot-tall banana plant, Norman looked around suspiciously. He didn't see any bats nearby, so he stepped up for a closer look.

The banana leaves were four feet long. Michael was interested to see a new leaf on top that had not opened yet. It was rolled like a long tube and stood straight up. It reminded him of Stanley and Fluffy's much smaller curled-up ice-cream-cone-shaped leaves that they used for sucking in socks.

Other plants had leaves so big that Dad said they would make good umbrellas. A sign explained that many medicines have been discovered in rain forest plants.

"This is cool," said Norman, "going for a walk in a rain forest!"

"Yeah, cool," said Max.

Dad said, "Real rain forests don't have paved paths."

Mom added, "Or gift shops and snack bars and rest rooms. But this *is* wonderful."

The path led to a gigantic kapok tree trunk. An opening in the side led to a metal spiral staircase for climbing to the upper floor. Mom and Dad took the regular stairs, while the kids scampered up inside the tree. At a hole halfway up, they stopped to look down into the greenery.

"Even though this tree must be fake," remarked Michael, "it looks really real."

Sarah said, "A real kapok tree wouldn't fit in a building. And cutting the inside out to put stairs in would kill it."

Norman said, "This is the best part so far."

"Yeah," agreed Max.

When they got to the upper floor, Norman and Max stopped at a drinking fountain because they were getting thirsty.

Back home, Fluffy was feeling thirsty, too. In the rush of leaving for Elmsville, Norman had forgotten to water him. The plant poked a vine under Norman's bed and dragged out the Water Blaster. He tried to aim it at the dirt in his pot but missed. Splat! He quivered a little in surprise at the gooey feel of syrup on his leaves. He tried again. Splat! More goo oozed over him. After two more splats, he figured out that he was not going to get any water as usual out of the Blaster. He began pulling himself out of the room—leaving little sticky spots of syrup on everything his vines touched as he went.

Chapter 11

The second level of the rain forest was divided into separate areas for many animals, most behind glass, with a few open sections. The signs showed where they were from—the Amazon River area in South America, and Malaysia in southeast Asia. A small clouded leopard snoozed on a ledge. A huge black long-haired anteater with an enormous long, pointed snout trotted across its space. Monkeys sitting together in treetops stared back at the people staring at them. A giant squirrel, the size of a small dog, with black and cinnamon-brown fur, scurried along a rock.

The fishing cat's area had a little pool where her next meal, several fish, swam. Some birds were behind glass, but others flew free in the open spaces. The brilliant blue, red, and yellow feathers of a macaw parrot were easy to spot in a small tree.

Norman and Max hurried ahead to the high glass wall

where the orangutans were. The apes were covered with long, shaggy red hair except for their faces. One was relaxing up in a leafless tree thirty feet high with thick vines for swinging.

"The tree must be fake," said Michael. Sarah nodded.

The largest orangutan, a male, was about as big as a short human and looked powerful. He was strolling about on all fours, leaning forward on the knuckles of his hands. A smaller female sat right next to the glass, people-watching. Her small brown eyes followed their every move.

Norman put his hand against the glass. He smiled and waved at her. The orangutan looked at him, looked away, and then stared at him. She lifted a long, graceful hand and placed it against his on the glass.

"She likes me!" exclaimed Norman.

The next part of the rain forest exhibit was so dimly lighted that it seemed like walking into a movie theater until their eyes got used to the dark. Around the walls were small and large lighted windows that showed creatures in what looked like natural habitats—with rocks, plants, water, and branches.

All four kids were very interested in the little poison frogs. One was bright blue, another coral, and another a pattern of black and neon yellow-green.

"I never saw anything like that before," remarked Sarah.

"Me either," agreed Michael.

Mom joked, "If you ever meet a blue frog, don't kiss it. Any of these are sure not to turn into a prince or princess."

Norman turned to glance at the opposite wall. The windows there were wide and so dark he couldn't see what was in there. He saw something swoop by.

"Look, more birds," he said.

Sarah looked. "No," she said. "Bats."

Norman took two steps backward. Sarah looked at the sign.

"Fruit bats," she read aloud. "Could be banana bats," she added, just to make Norman squirm.

Everyone but Norman moved close to the dark windows to peer in.

The branches of several small wide trees were festooned with bats hanging upside down. Their wings were folded close to their grayish-brown bodies. Every few moments, one would take off and flap to another branch. With wings spread, they looked much bigger while flying. One bat hung from the grid of an air vent in the ceiling by one foot and scratched an itch with the other.

"I've never seen a bat close up before," said Mom. "They're really interesting, aren't they?"

Michael thought their pointed faces with bright beady eyes and pointed ears looked like foxes. Max bent his head way over to try to see what the bats would look like right side up.

Dad remarked, "If they can see us, I bet they think *we're* upside down."

Sarah said, "They're kind of cute."

Norman stepped up to the glass. He was surprised to see that she was right. Suddenly there was a man walking inside the bat exhibit. He was wearing a tan zoo uniform and carrying three open metal containers.

"Who's that?" asked Max.

"Batman," said Norman. Everybody laughed with him. He was starting to feel less squeamish about bats.

Mom said, "That looks like cut-up fruit in those containers."

"Bat food," said Norman. The man hung the containers behind tree limbs, where they could not be seen from the windows. Bats started flying over to get food and back to the other trees to eat.

They moved on to look at other amazing creatures. It took them awhile to spot the walkingstick insect because it looked exactly like a stick, only with legs. They saw leaf cutter ants at work, small snakes, and weird lizards. A giant python coiled like an enormous garden hose, with a beautiful black and brown pattern on its skin, was not moving.

"Is it real?" asked Norman.

"Is it dead?" asked Max.

Dad replied, "I'm sure it's real. I read somewhere that pythons don't move much for days after they've eaten. Maybe it's digesting a big meal."

"What do they eat?" asked Max.

"Probably something large," said Dad.

"Definitely not fruit," said Michael.

Mom said, "I don't think we want to know the details right now. Not when we're going to be eating lunch soon. You can look it up when we get home."

The huge crocodile, ten feet long, which they came to next, wasn't moving either.

"He ate a big meal, too?" asked Max.

"Probably," said Dad. "Or he just needed a nap."

The crocodile was stretched out in water by the glass,

so they were standing right next to it and could see the bumps all over its hide.

A flash of light and the sound of thunder attracted them to a display that wasn't behind glass. A little jungle of mangrove trees was surrounded by water like a moat and fenced off by a railing. Large lizards sat around on rocks under the trees. A wind stirred the leaves. They could feel it blowing. Suddenly rain began pouring, a torrent splashing into the water. More lightning flashed and thunder rumbled. Michael craned his neck to see where the rain was coming from. It was a curtain of water pouring from holes in a long, curved pipe high above. Only the tips of the branches hanging over the water were actually getting wet.

"A fake storm!" he exclaimed. "This is great!"

When the rain stopped, the little jungle brightened as if the sun had come out. A heavy mist rose from the water. The kids all liked the storm so much that they hurried back later to see it again two more times. They finally figured out that the trees and everything else were fake except the water and the lizards. This amazed them even more.

Dr. Sparks caught up with them later while they were eating lunch at the zoo's main snack bar.

She reported, "The rain forest botanists have decided they don't need the kongabonga after all."

"What's going to happen to it?" asked Mom.

"The research center doesn't want it back," replied Dr. Sparks. "Would you like to keep it?"

Mom shook her head. "We can't handle any more plants. We have our hands full with Stanley and Fluffy. What about giving it to the plant auction?"

"That's an excellent idea," said Dr. Sparks. "Could you take it with you and deliver it to them? Take the rolling platform, too."

"Sure," said Dad. "No problem. We'll drop it off at McDougall's on the way home."

After lunch they went to the zoo's gift shop. Sarah picked out a T-shirt with a macaw on it. Norman chose a yellow-green plastic snake like one they had seen at the rain forest, so Max had to get one, too. Since Sarah wasn't looking when he picked it out, he used it to startle his sister. Michael chose an orangutan key ring.

They spent the rest of the day strolling through the zoo, looking at giraffes, elephants, lions, flamingos, seals, and many other creatures. Around every turn they saw something wonderful. Dad used up several rolls of film.

After the two families said goodbye in the parking lot, Michael and Norman were crammed into the back seat with the homeless kongabonga between them.

They had not driven very far before Norman started whining, "Can we keep this plant? Please, please, please?"

"No," said Mom firmly. "Someone who loves plants will buy it at the auction and give it a good home."

"But she'd rather live at our house," continued Norman.

"No more plants," ordered Dad. "No arguing. Case closed."

Mom asked Norman, "Why are you calling this one a she?"

"She's a girl plant," he replied.

"Why do you think that?"

"I just think it," Norman said.

Michael looked out the window, daydreaming. The tip of a curly vine brushed against his nose. He pushed it away.

A little later Norman burst out giggling. "Stop it!" he exclaimed.

Mom said without turning around, "Michael, quit bothering your brother!"

"I'm not doing anything," said Michael. "I didn't even touch him."

Dad glanced in the rearview mirror. "What's going on back there?" he asked.

Norman giggled again. "She's tickling me! On my nose!"

Mom turned and saw that a curly vine was touching Norman's face.

"Your face is in the way," said Mom. "Move your head over."

"She's tickling me again," said Norman.

Mom said, "She's not doing it on purpose."

"She likes me," said Norman.

Michael singsonged, "Norman's got a girlfriend. Only she's a plant."

Norman bragged, "I already have three girlfriends. People ones." He reeled off their names and added, "Bob only has two."

Mom said, "This is the first I've heard of this. How do you feel about having three girlfriends?"

"It makes me sort of happy," replied Norman with a smile.

Dad asked, "How do you know they're your girlfriends? Did they tell you they like you?"

"One did," said Norman. "The rest I just know like me."

Michael said scornfully, "He thinks any girl who says hello to him is his girlfriend."

"I do not!" said Norman. "I can tell."

"How?"

"I just know. How many girlfriends have *you* got?"

Michael mumbled, "None of your business."

Dad said, "Knock it off, Norman, this isn't a contest."

Michael said, "You thought the orangutan liked you, too. That makes four girlfriends."

"She's not my girlfriend," replied Norman. "We're just friends. I think Sarah likes you."

"No, she doesn't," said Michael.

"She's always talking to you."

Michael replied, "She's always trying to show off that she thinks she knows more about plants than I do."

"Well, she *does* know more," said Norman.

"Does not!"

"Does too!"

Dad turned up the radio full blast.

When they got back to their town, it was early evening, past closing time at McDougall Plants. They stopped by anyway, on the chance that someone might be there, but the place was locked.

"We'll have to deliver the plant tomorrow," said Dad.

"Yay!" said Norman. "She gets to sleep over at our house one more night!"

Chapter 12

On the way home, they dropped off their rolls of film to be developed. Dad ordered double prints so they could send a set to the Sparkses.

When they came into the house, they heard water running in the bathroom.

"Could a pipe have broken?" asked Mom.

Dad asked Norman, "You didn't put any more peat pots down the drain, did you?"

"Not me," said Norman.

They found the shower running. Norman's empty Blaster was in the bathtub. Fluffy stood next to the tub, amid many puddles of water. Wet towels were strewn about the room.

"Uh-oh," said Norman.

"It looks like he was trying to take a shower," said Michael.

"'Why?" asked Mom.

Norman said, "He must have tried to water himself with my Blaster. But it had maple syrup in it. So he had to wash the goo off."

Mom told Norman, "Your plant, your Blaster, your cleanup."

Norman sighed and went to work.

They put the guest plant back in the dining room for the night. Norman wanted to keep it in the boys' room. That way, he explained, they would be having a real sleepover. But Dad said no, if the visitor was around Fluffy and Stanley when they were eating socks, it might get ideas.

Mom called Mrs. Smith about donating the plant for the auction. She came right over to look at it.

"This is wonderful!" she exclaimed. "How nice of Susan to give this for our big event."

Norman said, "I'm trying to think of a good name for her."

Mrs. Smith looked puzzled. "Who?" she asked. "Susan Sparks?"

"No, this plant," he said.

"What kind is it?"

"A kongabonga."

"Then you could call it Konga. Or Bonga."

"I want a girl name," said Norman. "It's a girl plant."

"How do you know that?"

"I just know it," he assured her.

Mrs. Smith smiled. "It used to be popular to name girls after plants. A lot of girls were called Rose, Lily, Ivy, Daisy, Fern, Iris, and Violet. And Porky Pig in the

74

old movie cartoons had a pig girlfriend named Petunia. Maybe you could choose one of those."

"I don't know," said Norman. "I could call her Rose if she had thorns, but she doesn't."

"If you want a cute name, you could name her after the Busy Lizzie plant."

Norman chuckled. "Is that a real plant?"

"Yes."

He thought over this suggestion. "I don't know," he said. "She doesn't do anything, so she isn't busy."

"You could just call her Lizzie."

"Like short for lizard? She doesn't look like a lizard."

"No, Lizzie is one of the nicknames for Elizabeth."

Norman touched one of the plant's curling vines.

"Curly," he decided. "I'm calling her Curly."

"Like in the Three Stooges?" asked Mrs. Smith.

"No, like curly vines. See? She's got them all over."

"Good idea," agreed Mrs. Smith. "All those curls remind me of the child movie star Shirley Temple. Have you seen any of her old movies?"

"I saw one," said Norman. "She sang and danced. She has lots of curls. All over her head. That can be Curly's last name—Curly Temple."

Late that night, long after the family was asleep, Stanley and Fluffy did their schlurping and burping and pulled themselves out of the boys' room. As they were running themselves around, towed by the remote control trucks, Stanley rolled into the dining room and bumped into the overnight guest. He tapped Curly with a vine as if to get her attention. One of her vines waved a little

75

as if to say hi. Then they gave each other a vine hand-shake. Fluffy rustled his leaves. Curly rustled back. They stood there awhile, doing nothing.

Stanley took hold of the rope handle on the rolling platform. He twisted some levers on his truck's remote control, and slowly towed himself and Curly into the kitchen. On they went, into the hall, and back around through the living room, dining room and kitchen. Around and around they went, faster and faster. Fluffy pulled himself into a corner of the living room to get out of the way.

Stanley slowed to a stop in the living room by the closet door. He put the control down on Curly's platform while he turned the door handle. He was still holding on to the truck. Curly poked at the control and twisted it, sending the truck and Stanley zooming away at top speed, jerking in one direction, then another. His pot smacked into a sharp corner of the coffee table so hard that it cracked. Soil began leaking out.

Stanley snatched the control back. He and Fluffy put their trucks away and rolled themselves back to the boys' room, leaving Curly in the living room.

Early in the morning Michael heard Norman saying, "Put your vines down against your sides. Like this. No, like this. Good. Now try to lean over." When he bent over to try to teach Fluffy to bow, he noticed the little trail of dirt between Stanley and the door. He looked in the hall and saw the longer dirt trail. Following it, he found Curly in the living room.

"Uh-oh," he said. He went back to check on Stanley. When he saw the broken pot, he poked his brother.

"Leave me alone," Michael mumbled.

To wake him up, Norman did a karate yell right in his ear: "Hi! Yaaah!"

Michael sat up suddenly like a character in a pop-up book. "What? What?"

"Stanley's pot got broke," explained Norman. "He leaked dirt all over. And I found Curly in the living room."

"Uh-oh," said Michael, sliding out of bed. "Let's get things fixed up before Mom and Dad wake up."

But Norman's yell had already alerted them.

"Now what!" exclaimed Dad in the doorway. Mom looked at the trail of dirt that led to Stanley.

"What happened to his pot?" she asked.

"I don't know," said Michael. "He must have had an accident."

Norman said, "Curly was in the living room, but she's okay."

Mom wondered, "I know this is a ridiculous thought, but you don't suppose she got in there on her own, do you?"

Michael replied, "I don't think she could pull herself around. Stanley or Fluffy must have done it. They were probably just playing."

"Whatever happened," said Dad, "I'm glad we're getting that plant out of here today. After that, it can do whatever it wants and it won't be our problem."

They all gathered around Stanley, trying to figure out if his pot could be fixed. While they weren't looking, Fluffy pressed his vines to his sides and bent his main stalk over, just a little bit.

Chapter 13

After breakfast Dad helped Michael tape the broken edges of Stanley's pot together.

"When we go to the greenhouse today," said Mom, "we'll take Stanley, too, and get him a new pot."

Mom took Curly to the greenhouse in the car, along with Norman. Michael tied a rope around the bottom of Stanley's main stalk and towed him with his bicycle, pedaling slowly.

Mom told Mr. McDougall, "Our friend Susan Sparks is donating this kongabonga to the auction. Barbara Smith said they'd be glad to accept it."

He looked it over. "I've never seen one of these before," he said.

Norman said, "Her name is Curly."

"Like in the Three Stooges?" asked Mr. McDougall.

"No, Curly Temple."

"Ah," said Mr. McDougall. "Because of the curly vines?"

"Yes," said Norman.

Mr. McDougall told Mom, "Would you ask Dr. Sparks to send us some information about it? Like where it's from and instructions for taking care of it."

"Of course," said Mom. "Now we need a new pot for one of our plants."

He looked at Stanley. "What happened here?" he asked. "These plastic ones are hard to break."

Michael said, "He had an accident. We didn't see it happen."

"That's strange," remarked Mr. McDougall.

After Stanley was settled in his new pot and Mom paid for it, Mr. McDougall took Curly on his lap. "I'll run this back to the auction section," he said. He glided away in the wheelchair. One of Curly's vines fell on his hand that was operating the control. He brushed it away.

Michael did not notice Stanley behind him lifting a vine as if to wave goodbye.

He said, "I wonder who's going to buy her."

"Not us," replied Mom.

On the way home, Stanley, rolling downhill, gained speed. Michael pedaled slower to let the plant pass him. When Stanley got the full rope's length ahead, Michael coasted, letting Stanley tow the bike for a while.

Shortly after Mom and Norman got home, the phone rang. It was Officer Tim.

"We just got a call about a large plant zooming down Oak Street. I'm checking with you first because all the plants-on-the-loose reports we've ever gotten turned out to be yours.''

Mom explained, ''Michael's towing his plant home with a rope tied to his bike. He's coming from McDougall's greenhouse at the top of Oak Street. That must be what someone saw.''

''The person who called didn't say anything about a bike,'' said Officer Tim.

The door opened and Michael came in pushing Stanley.

Mom said, ''They just got home. They're okay.'' She asked Michael, ''Did you let Stanley get away from you going downhill?''

''No, I just let him run ahead a little,'' he admitted.

''I told you not to do that!''

''But he was tied with the rope the whole time!''

Mom explained again to Officer Tim that the plant had been tied to the bike. She promised that they would be careful not to cause any more runaway plant reports.

When they got the developed pictures back, Norman hung over Dad's arm to look at them.

''Where are the ones I took?'' he asked.

Michael said, ''Look for the ones with no heads and all feet.''

Dad said, ''Here are the group pictures that you're not in, so they must be the ones you took. They have heads this time. Good job.''

Norman asked, ''What's this one? It doesn't look like anything.''

''That must be the one you took of your fingers,'' said Dad.

"Oh, yeah," said Norman.

"Here's another strange one," said Dad. "Did you take this? Were you fooling around with the camera when you weren't supposed to?"

Norman looked at the print. "Nope. What's that supposed to be?"

"I'm not sure. It's out of focus, very fuzzy. It looks like part of the kitchen wall and ceiling. And this one," Dad continued, "is a picture of the kitchen floor with part of a table leg. Here's the handle of the refrigerator, a view of the sink slanting uphill, two shots of the bottom of the stove, and the floor again."

Mom asked, "What's this here in the floor picture?"

Norman said, "It looks like the back of a remote control truck."

"Did you leave yours in the kitchen?"

"I always put it away in the closet."

"Well, *somebody* left it in the kitchen. Somebody who was fooling around with the camera when he wasn't supposed to."

"Not me," said Norman.

"It wasn't me," said Michael. "I know how to take pictures so you can tell what they are."

Dad looked through the mysterious fuzzy kitchen pictures again. "These look like they were taken by someone who never used a camera before." He checked the numbers on the negatives. "Aha!" he said. "The kitchen pictures were taken after the ones in the dining room and before the zoo ones." He and Mom turned to look at Norman.

"You and Max were horsing around that night," said Mom. "Did you let Max play with the camera?"

"No!" replied Norman. "We were only doing karate and the Hokey Pokey."

Dad said, "These pictures look like whoever took them might have been doing the Hokey Pokey at the same time."

"We didn't!" protested Norman.

"Then that leaves . . ." began Dad.

"Aha!" said Michael. "Leaves! It must have been Stanley or Fluffy."

"Great," said Dad. "Thanks to your plants, I just paid for wasted film and developing of fourteen fuzzy pictures of kitchen parts. With double prints!"

"Maybe Dr. Sparks'll like them," suggested Michael. They're probably the only pictures in the world taken by a plant."

Mom pointed out, "At least in the ones Norman took everybody has a head. Except for the fingers one. He's making progress."

Early the next morning, Norman was in a singing mood. He quietly started doing the Hokey Pokey. Fluffy joined in, putting vines in and out. Norman noticed that when Fluffy reached out a vine, it looked like he was doing sort of a punch, only very slowly.

Norman started singing faster, Fluffy reached vines out faster. Norman sang still faster, adding lots of "Hi! Ahs!" to the song. He was so excited that he got louder and louder. This woke Michael.

Seeing Norman and Fluffy doing the Hokey Pokey at practically warp speed, he exclaimed, "What are you doing!"

"It's karate!" yelled Norman. "When we do the Hokey Pokey real fast, it's just like karate! Hi! Ah!"

Fluffy was thrusting vines out very fast in several directions.

The door opened. Dad said, "I told you not to yell 'Hi! Ah!' in the morning. What are you doing!"

Norman flopped, exhausted, on his bed. Fluffy dropped his vines and stood sagging on his skateboard.

Michael explained, "They just invented a new dance—the Hokey Karate."

While they ate breakfast, the front doorbell rang. It was Officer Tim.

"Come in," said Dad. "It's nice to see you. I hope nothing's wrong."

"I'm just checking out a weird call," replied Officer Tim. "The officers on the overnight shift didn't have time to follow it up. They had bigger problems to deal with. But things were quiet when I came on duty this morning, and I was in the neighborhood. So I thought I'd just check it out with you."

"We haven't been involved in anything weird *lately*," said Dad. "Come on in the kitchen and have some coffee."

"What's going on?" asked Mom.

Officer Tim explained, "We're used to weird calls, but one last night was a doozie. About two A.M. somebody reported seeing a speeding wheelchair on Oak Street."

Dad asked, "What's wrong with someone in a wheelchair being in a hurry? Whoever it was wasn't likely to run over anybody on the sidewalk late at night."

83

"The wheelchair wasn't on the sidewalk. It was in the street. And there wasn't anybody sitting in it."

Norman said, "Maybe it's a haunted wheelchair! Maybe an invisible ghost was running it!"

"No, there was something real sitting in it all right," said Officer Tim. "It was a plant."

Chapter 14

"We're sure it wasn't one of ours," said Mom, looking at the boys. "We *are* sure, aren't we?" They nodded.

Michael said, "It couldn't have been one of ours. Our plants can't sit down."

Officer Tim said, "You understand, of course, that I'm checking with you because your house has always turned out to be headquarters for plants on the loose."

Norman suggested, "Maybe it was a person dressed up like a plant. Like in that movie about the Swamp Monster that was partly a plant. It was special effects, not a real monster. It was really a guy in a green glop suit. Maybe last night it was a guy in a plant suit."

Officer Tim laughed and shook his head. "It's very unlikely that anybody wearing a plant suit would be speeding down Oak Street in a wheelchair at two in the morning."

Norman said, "Maybe his plant suit was too tight so he couldn't walk fast and that's why he was riding a wheelchair. Or maybe his feet got stuck in a flowerpot."

Dad smiled and said, "He should have called his parents to come pick him up."

Norman added, "Maybe he couldn't call his mom and dad to come and get him because he was supposed to be home by midnight like Cinderella, and they'd be mad because he was late, and his fairy godmother got mixed up, so his coach turned into a wheelchair instead of a pumpkin, and his clothes turned into a plant suit."

Officer Tim asked Mom, "Is he like this all the time?"

"Fairly often," said Mom.

"Amazing, isn't he?" said Dad. Norman beamed with pride and went back to finishing his cereal.

Michael asked, "Do you know what the speeding plant looked like?"

"The driver who reported it said he was stopped at a red light. He saw in his rearview mirror that it was coming up behind his car. He got a quick look as it whizzed by his window. He said it was very leafy, about three feet high, in a large pot on the seat of the wheelchair. He thought some vines appeared to be wrapped around the chair arm, but he wasn't sure. It happened so fast."

He continued, "I know your plants are taller than that, but I wondered if you might have gotten a new shorter one."

"Nope," said Norman. "I thought about getting a Venus' flytrap, but Mom wouldn't let me. It's a meat-eater. Bugs."

"Good decision," said Officer Tim. "Judging by the other two plants you've raised, if you got a meat-eater, it'd probably grow huge, get tired of bugs, and start going out by itself for hamburgers at McDonald's."

Norman giggled.

Dad asked, "Have any wheelchairs been reported stolen?"

"Not yet," replied Officer Tim.

Michael said, "We know somebody who's got a wheelchair and a lot of plants." They told him about Mr. McDougall.

"We'll check it out," said Officer Tim.

Michael asked, "Did you catch the vandals yet who messed up our playground?"

"Not yet. There have been two more incidents with broken glass and the same kind of spray paint. Last night at a vacant building they broke windows instead of bottles."

As Officer Tim went out the front door, Mrs. Smith came in to find out why a police car was in their driveway.

The next morning Officer Tim came by again.

"Are you sure your plants weren't out last night?"

Dad asked, "What's up? Was the one in the wheel-chair running around again?"

"Yes, and two more were spotted sailing down Oak Street—one in a shopping cart, and another one rolling on a desk chair with wheels."

Michael said, "The greenhouse has both of those things."

Norman said, "Stanley or Fluffy wouldn't use a shopping cart or a desk chair. They have their skateboards."

Mom asked, "Did you get descriptions?"

"Just about what the plants were riding in. The people who saw them were so surprised that they didn't get a good look."

"Did you check with Mr. McDougall at the greenhouse?" asked Mom.

"I talked with him yesterday. Nothing was missing— not his wheelchair, not any plants. Although there are so many plants there, I don't know how he could tell if any were gone. But when he arrived for work, he thought his wheelchair wasn't where he'd left it. But he wasn't sure. We'll check there again."

Michael asked, "Were the plants rolling on the part of Oak Street that slopes down?"

"They were seen on the flat stretch," said Officer Tim. "If they came from the higher part of Oak, they'd be going fast when they got to the flat part, but they'd eventually slow to a stop. They couldn't roll back uphill, so maybe we'll find them near where they stopped— unless somebody saw them and decided 'Finders keepers.'"

Michael said, "The shopping cart and chair couldn't roll back uphill, but the wheelchair could. It's got battery-powered controls."

"You think a plant was running the wheelchair?"

"I don't know," said Michael. "But some plants can do amazing things."

Norman said, "Maybe it was Curly Temple."

"Shirley Temple?" asked Officer Tim, looking baffled. "The old kid movie star? This sounds more like something the Little Rascals would be mixed up in."

"No, *Curly* Temple. She's a girl plant," explained Norman. "She slept over at our house two nights."

Officer Tim asked Mom, "What on earth is he talking about?"

She said, "Norman, let's not get into that right now. Officer Tim is a busy man."

"Yes," said Officer Tim. "I have to get back to work."

As he was going out the door, Mrs. Smith arrived to see why a police car was in front of their house again.

"Where do you suppose those plants could have been trying to go?" wondered Dad.

Norman suggested, "Maybe one was Curly—trying to come over to our house to visit me and Fluffy and Stanley."

Michael said, "Maybe they weren't going anywhere special—just having fun rolling downhill—like sledding or skiing or riding a rollercoaster."

Mom said, "If Curly Temple really is one of those running around, we can't let an out-of-control plant be sold at the auction."

Michael suggested, "Let's go over to the greenhouse after school to see what we can find out."

"Okay," she agreed. "Then I'm calling Susan about this."

At the greenhouse Mr. McDougall was using his wheelchair, but he said two plants, a shopping cart, and the desk chair were still missing. The police had not found any sign of a break-in.

"Where's Curly?" asked Norman.

"Who?" asked Mr. McDougall.

"The plant with the curly vines," explained Mom. "The kongabonga Susan Sparks donated. Norman calls it Curly."

"It's in the back, with the other auction plants," he said. "But we found it up front here with the wheelchair this morning. Somebody put plants on things with wheels and gave them a push downhill. But the police haven't figured out how they got in or why they brought the wheelchair back. All the keys are accounted for, and all my employees can be trusted."

Mom asked, "Do you suppose it could have been the vandals who've been damaging things around town?"

Mr. McDougall replied, "The police don't think so because those creeps like to break glass. This whole building is mostly glass, and nothing's broken. But the police have a plan to find out what's happening. A couple of officers are going to hide here tonight and watch so they can catch whoever's doing it."

"Can we come watch, too?" asked Norman.

"No," said Mom.

Michael and Norman went back to see Curly. She looked fine.

Norman said, "I think it was her."

Michael agreed, "I do, too. It probably wasn't a break-*in* by people. I think it was a break*out* by plants. Three of them got out last night, and Curly was the only one that came back."

Late that night as the family slept, Stanley reached over from his regular spot beside Michael's bed and pulled Michael's covers up to his chin. Fluffy checked Norman's covers and patted him on the head. Soon the

90

plants began to reach for their dinners. They schlurped. They burped. Fluffy said, ''Ex'' after every burp. As they finished the last of their socks, there was a thump outside—as if something had bumped into the house. Then there was a tapping on the window.

Chapter 15

At first Stanley and Fluffy paid no attention. They kept on digesting their meals. The noise at the window got a little louder. Tap. Tap! TAP!!! Stanley pressed a vine against the glass as if to feel what was on the other side.

The noise got louder. Bang. Bang! BANG!!! This woke Michael. In the dim light from the hall, he saw Stanley pulling out of the room. Michael slid out of bed and turned on his lamp. Through the window, he saw a garden trowel banging on the glass. He was barely able to see what was holding it—a curly, green vine.

Michael ran across the hall to wake Dad and Mom. Then he dashed after Stanley. By the time he got to the living room, his plant had gotten a remote control truck from the closet, unlocked the front door and was zooming out.

"Stanley!" yelled Michael. "Stop! Come back!"

Dad and Mom were right behind him. Behind them came Fluffy and Norman.

"Fluffy pulled me out of bed," said Norman, very bewildered. "What's happening?"

"Curly was banging on the window," explained Michael, "and Stanley took off outside."

"She must like Stanley," said Norman. "She's his girlfriend."

"Great," said Mom. "I hope they haven't gone out on a date."

Dad said, "I can just picture them sitting in the back row at the movies, holding vines. We have to go look for them. They can't have gone far."

A familiar voice outside called, "We got the one with the wheelchair! And another one—with a—what *is* this? A toy truck?" Officer Tim and his partner came up the front walk pulling Stanley and pushing Curly.

"Thank you," said Dad, helping them bring the plants in.

Officer Tim said, "I knew when there were plants on the loose, one of them would turn out to be yours."

Michael said, "Mine wasn't running around swiping wheelchairs. He wouldn't have gone out if Curly hadn't come over and banged on the window."

"Since she likes to wander so much, you should change her name to Wanda," Officer Tim suggested.

"I like that name," said Norman. "I'm going to call her Wanda. Curly can be her middle name. Wanda Curly Temple."

Michael asked Officer Tim, "Did she get out of the greenhouse by herself?"

"Yes, how did you know?"

"We figured it out," bragged Norman.

Officer Tim remarked, "I wouldn't have believed it unless I saw it. We decided to follow this plant instead of grabbing it right away. We wanted to find out where it was going."

"Look," said Michael, pointing at Wanda Curly. "She brought a friend." Tucked in behind her on the wheelchair seat was a small potted plant.

Mom laughed. "Maybe she brought the friend for Fluffy, for a double date."

Officer Tim said, "I never heard of plants having dates."

Norman could not resist making a joke. "Some plants have dates," he said. "The palm trees that grow them."

Officer Tim said, "I've got a plant joke for you. Knock, knock."

"Who's there?" asked Norman.

"Wanda."

"Wanda who?"

"Wanda lock up your plant so it won't get out of the house?"

"My plant didn't do anything," said Norman. "I don't wanda lock him up." He chuckled.

Officer Tim started pushing Wanda Curly and her little friend out the door.

"Are you taking them back to the greenhouse?" asked Michael.

"In the morning," said Officer Tim. "They'll spend the night at the police station."

As Officer Tim left, Michael heard him say to his partner, "Maybe we should try to get the city council to pass a curfew law for plants. Then we could arrest them if they were out late."

His partner replied, "Only if you want to get us laughed out of town."

The phone rang. "Who could be calling at this time of night?" Dad said. It was Mrs. Smith, wondering what a police car was doing at their house *again*.

Mom called Susan Sparks in the morning with the news abut Curly. She was amazed and said she'd better take the plant back to study it. She would come and pick it up herself because she wanted to find out first-hand about what the plant had done.

"As long as you're coming, why don't you bring the whole family and stay for the auction?" Mom suggested. "We'd love to have you here again."

Dr. Sparks called back to say she would bring a different plant for the auction and to get them four tickets because her husband could come along this time.

Mom called Mr. McDougall to tell him Susan Sparks would pick up the kongabonga when she came for the auction. "I hope it won't get out of your greenhouse again before then," she said.

"It won't be going anywhere," he said. "I grounded it until we could figure out what to do with it."

"How do you ground a plant?" Mom asked.

"I planted it in ground," he said, "inside like the climbing rose."

Mom laughed. "Too bad that wouldn't work with kids," she said.

When Michael found out Sarah was coming to visit again, he went to the library to get some plant books. He was going to need more facts.

In the days that followed, Norman went around telling knock-knock jokes to anyone who would listen. He was driving his family crazy.

Finally Mom gave up and joined in. One night when they were having pizza for dinner, she said, "Knock, knock."

"Who's there?" asked Norman and Michael together.

"Wanda."

"We already know that one," said Norman.

"No, you don't," said Mom. "Say 'Wanda who?' "

"Wanda who?" asked Dad.

Mom replied, "Wanda 'nother piece of pizza?"

"Yes!" they all shouted.

Michael was getting tired of Norman's jokes. So he told him one of his own.

"Knock, knock," he said.

"Who's there?" replied Norman.

"Nobody."

"Nobody who?" Michael did not reply.

"Nobody who?" repeated Norman. Michael said nothing.

"Say who!" demanded Norman.

Michael replied, smiling smugly, "If nobody's there, nobody answers. Gotcha!"

Norman scowled at Michael. Then he went over to Bob's house to fool him with the nobody joke.

Chapter 16

Early on the evening of the auction, the truck came to pick up Stanley and Fluffy to deliver them to the hotel.

"I'll see you there," Michael murmured to Stanley so that the guys loading the plants would not hear.

Norman kept looking out the living room window to see if the Sparkses' van was coming down the street yet. Mom got all dressed up in a green dress. Dad put on his best suit.

Mom told the boys, "Hurry up and get dressed for the party. Good pants, good shirt, tie, dark socks, no sneakers. Move! The Sparkses will be here soon."

For once Michael did not have to be nagged to get dressed up. As he put on the dark brown socks that went with his good brown pants, he said to Stanley, "You're getting chocolate for dinner tonight."

Norman put on dark blue socks that matched his good blue pants. "Mine are blueberry," he said.

They heard a burst of loud voices from the front of the house. The Sparkses had arrived. Norman dashed down the hall to see Max. Michael tied the laces of his good brown shoes and carefully brushed his hair. Then he strolled out of the room, trying to look casual.

Coming through the hall was a thundering herd of four Sparkses, wearing their usual jeans, T-shirts, and sneakers and carrying travel bags. He pressed himself against the wall to let them by.

"Hi, Michael," said Fred Sparks. "We have to do a quick change." They fanned out into the bathroom and bedrooms to put on their party clothes. Michael went out to look in the van to see the new plant they had brought.

In a few minutes, Sarah came outside looking very nice in a blue dress. She had tied her hair back with a red ribbon.

"Where are Stanley and Fluffy?" she asked.

"They already went ahead to the party in a truck. Mrs. Smith wanted them to be on display."

Soon everyone was ready to go. The fathers decided that eight people would not fit comfortably in the van with a large plant already in it, so Dad would also drive his car. Norman insisted on going with Max in the van.

As Mr. Sparks closed the van door, Michael heard Norman saying, "Knock, knock."

"Okay, have we got everything?" asked Dad. He patted his pockets to be sure he had his keys and wallet.

Mom said, "I've got the camera and extra film in my purse. We're all set."

On the way to the hotel, Michael enjoyed having the whole backseat to himself without Norman bothering him.

*　　*　　*

The parking lot was almost full.

"Looks like a good turnout," said Dad.

"I hope this raises a lot of money," said Mom. "Barbara and the other committee members have worked so hard on this."

A sign in the hotel lobby pointed to the huge room full of dressed-up people where the party was being held. Mrs. Smith was there to greet them. She told Mr. Sparks where to check in the plant.

Norman looked around. "Where's Fluffy and Stanley?" he asked.

"They're in the ballroom next door," she explained. "All the display and auction plants are in there."

"The ball room?" said Norman. "They have a room for playing ball?"

Mrs. Smith smiled. "No, a ball also means a dancing party. A big room that's used for dancing parties is called a ballroom. It has a smooth wooden floor that's easy to move your feet on. Come on, I'll show you. I know you want to check on your plants."

They went through a wide doorway. All around the walls plants stood on long tables. The big ones stood on the floor. Each plant had a sign with its name and facts about it. The auction plants also had numbers. Many of the people who donated them were there to tell about them for anyone interested.

Norman and Michael, trailed by Max, headed straight for Stanley and Fluffy. Both plants looked calm and contented to be there.

Norman slid one foot along the smooth wooden floor. "This *is* a good floor!" he said to Max. He ran a few steps and slid with both feet. Max did the same. Their mothers grabbed them.

"No sliding," said Mom sternly.

"You might knock somebody over," warned Dr. Sparks. "Come on, let's look at all the plants."

Mom noticed a piano and a set of drums in a corner.

"Is there going to be music for dancing?" she asked Mrs. Smith.

"No, a couple of musicians have volunteered to play before and during dinner—just background music."

Michael hoped they would not play the Hokey Pokey.

Norman spotted Mr. McDougall, who was getting around on his crutches, and went over to him. Max followed.

Norman asked him, "Is Wanda here?"

"Wanda who?"

Norman couldn't resist this unexpected opportunity. He replied, "Wanda 'nother piece of pizza?"

Mr. McDougall looked at him as if he had gone completely goofball. "Who's Wanda?" he asked. "And what pizza?"

Norman explained, "It's a knock-knock joke."

Mr. McDougall said, "For a knock-knock joke, aren't you supposed to start with knock-knock?"

"Yeah, but I decided to start in the middle 'cause you said 'Wanda who?' "

Mr. McDougall replied, "Tell me who Wanda is."

Max piped up, "You're supposed to say 'Wanda who?' "

"I already said that," said Mr. McDougall, "and look where it got me."

Norman explained, "Wanda is Curly. That's her new

name. Wanda Curly Temple. Did you bring her tonight, or is she still grounded?"

"She's at the greenhouse, but we ungrounded her today. We dug her up and repotted her to be ready for Dr. Sparks to pick up tomorrow morning."

The musicians started playing. Michael and Sarah followed their parents around, listening as people answered questions about plants. They were both trying to collect facts that they could one-up each other with.

They stopped to watch a television screen showing a video about the fourteen-foot cactus that needed a new home.

Many people gathered around a miniature model showing what the children's gardens would look like.

Mom took pictures of both families and Mrs. Smith with various plants in the background and the garden model. Then Dad took some so Mom could get in the pictures.

When it was time to eat, everyone went back to the other room. They helped themselves at long buffet tables with many choices of food. They carried their plates to smaller tables to eat.

Michael got up a couple of times to check on Stanley and Fluffy in the ballroom. They were fine. The musicians played lots of songs, but not the Hokey Pokey.

Chapter 17

After dinner, a man announced on a microphone, "The auction will begin in five minutes. Please take your seats." The crowd moved to rows of chairs in the same room where they had dinner.

Dad and Mr. Sparks went to find a quiet corner to talk sports while the auction was going on. Mrs. Smith escorted Dr. Sparks to the front row. Sarah went with her mother. Mom found seats for herself and the boys in the back row.

"Come sit closer to the front," urged Mrs. Smith.

"I want to sit back here," explained Mom, "so if the kids get fidgety, I can keep an eye on them."

When the crowd was seated, Mrs. Smith thanked everyone who had helped make the event a success. She made Dr. Sparks stand up and introduced her, too. Then she introduced the man who was running the auction.

"First," he said, "for anyone who has not bid in an

auction before, I want to explain briefly how this works. I will announce the name and number of each plant listed in your program. I'll suggest an amount for an opening bid. If you want to make that bid, raise your hand. If I don't see you immediately, wave to get my attention. From there on, you can speak up to make a higher bid. Or wait for me to ask for a higher amount and raise your hand. When we get the price up to where there are no more bids, I'll bang my gavel and the plant will be sold to the last bidder.

"After the sale, please see my assistant to pay. We take cash, checks, or credit cards. For the large plants too big for you to carry home tonight, we'll arrange to have them delivered tomorrow.

"This is for a very good cause, so bid high and bid often. Now, on to our first plant." He told details about it and began the auction. "May I have an opening bid of fifty dollars?"

A man in the front row raised his hand.

"Thank you. We have fifty dollars. Do I hear seventy-five?" Another hand went up.

"One hundred," said a woman seated in the middle of the crowd. She and the man in the front row went back and forth, bidding higher and higher.

"We have three hundred from the gentleman in the front row," said the auctioneer. "Do I hear three-fifty?"

The woman said nothing.

"Three hundred, going, going, gone," called the auctioneer. He banged the gavel. "Sold to the gentleman in the front row!"

As the auction went on, the boys got restless. Norman whispered to Mom that he had to go to the bathroom.

"Me, too," whispered Max.

She told Michael to take them to the men's room. Everyone in their row had to stand up to let them through, leaving Mom in the middle of the row.

When they came back, Michael walked up behind the row and whispered to Mom, "I'm tired of the auction. Can I go look at plants in the ballroom again?"

"Me, too," whispered Norman.

"Me, too," said Max.

"All right," agreed Mom, "but Michael, you have to watch Norman and Max."

"I don't want to."

"Then come back and sit down."

"Okay, I'll watch them," Michael said.

Some of the people sitting near them were glaring at them because of their loud whispering.

Mom watched the boys go through the large doorway, off to the side. From where she sat, she could see into part of the ballroom where the boys were walking around, behaving themselves. She turned her attention back to the auction.

The plant Susan Sparks had donated sold for one hundred dollars.

Later, when Mom glanced back towards the ballroom, Michael was standing in the doorway watching the auction. Behind his back, Norman slid by, going fast on the smooth floor. A moment later, Max slid by.

Instead of making everybody in the row stand up to let her out, Mom waved to get Michael's attention.

He didn't notice. Behind him, Norman and Max slid by again, going faster the other way. She waved faster at Michael. He still didn't see her.

Bang went the gavel. "Sold!" said the auctioneer, "to the lady in the back row!"

Mrs. Smith hurried over behind Mom's seat and patted her on the shoulder.

"I'm glad you changed your mind," she said. "But where on earth are you going to put it?"

"Put what?" asked Mom.

"The cactus."

"What cactus?"

"The fourteen-foot-tall one you just bought."

"I didn't!"

Mrs. Smith explained, "When the bid was seven hundred, the auctioneer asked for seven-fifty, but nobody said anything. He started to say 'Going, going, gone' but before he did, you raised your hand and started madly waving. Yours was the winning bid."

"Seven hundred and fifty dollars!" exclaimed Mom. "I wasn't bidding! I was waving at Michael to get him to make Norman and Max stop doing running slides in the ballroom."

"Oh, dear," said Mrs. Smith. "Let's see if we can straighten this out." She explained to the auctioneer's assistant that her friend had been waving to get her child to stop horsing around, not bidding.

The assistant said, "I understand. I have kids, too. Let me go find the next highest bidder." After talking with the man, she came back. "He'll take it for his last bid of seven hundred. He's happy to get it."

Mom rounded up the three boys. She got to Norman and Max just in time. They were starting to play with the piano, plunking notes with one finger. She herded them back to the other room and made them stand with her in the back to watch the auction.

After a while, from the ballroom came the sounds of someone plunking on the piano again—one key at a time—then a bunch of keys at once—the way little children bang on a keyboard.

Thump, thump, thump. Someone was also playing the drums. Crash went the cymbals. People were turning around to see what was going on. The auctioneer stopped talking. Mrs. Smith was hurrying over. Mom and the boys beat her to the ballroom door.

"Uh-oh," said Michael. Banging on the piano was Fluffy, backed by Stanley on drums.

Michael and Norman wheeled their plants away to the other end of the ballroom, where there was nothing for them to grab onto to pull themselves around. Michael pried the drumsticks out of Stanley's clutches.

As soon as the piano and drum noise stopped, the auctioneer went on. Everyone turned their attention back to the sale. Mom told the boys to watch Stanley and Fluffy to prevent any more surprises.

At the end of the auction, Mrs. Smith thanked everyone and announced that the event had raised about forty thousand dollars for the children's garden project.

People crowded into the ballroom to pick up the plants they had bought. Mr. McDougall was pointing out to his helpers which of the larger plants had to be loaded in the moving van. The boys helped roll Stanley and Fluffy out and saw them put safely in the truck. Then they went to find their parents.

Dr. Sparks was surrounded by a group asking her questions about botany. Mom was helping the auctioneer's assistant sort out the sales records. They found Dad, Mr. Sparks, and Sarah sitting in the lobby, watching party-goers leaving with plants they had bought.

Finally Mom and Susan Sparks came out.

"Ready to go?" asked Dad.

"Have you got the camera?" asked Mom.

"No, I thought you had it. Who had it last?"

Mom recalled, "I put it down on a table in the ballroom. I thought you picked it up because when I turned around it was gone."

They retraced their steps, but did not find it.

Mrs. Smith said, "Maybe someone turned it in at the desk in the lobby."

Dad asked there, but the camera had not been found. The manager promised she would have the cleanup people look for it.

Mr. McDougall walked slowly by on his crutches. "Oh, you're still here," he said. "I thought you'd gone. The truck's already left for the greenhouse. It was going to drop your plants at your house first."

"But we're not home," Norman pointed out.

"Don't worry," said Mr. McDougall. "When they find you're not home, they'll take yours back to the greenhouse for the night with the others."

"Maybe we can catch up with them," said Dad.

"You go ahead," said Mr. Sparks. "I'll take everybody home in the van."

Michael said to Dad, "I'm coming with you."

"Me, too," said Norman. Max wanted to go along, but his father said no.

Dad and the boys sprinted to the car. There was a full moon out, shining a bright and beautiful light. When they got home, they had missed the truck. A note on the front door said that the plants would be kept overnight at the greenhouse. They should call in the morning about what time to deliver them tomorrow.

Michael said, "Stanley and Fluffy can't stay there tonight. They don't have any socks to eat."

Norman added, "They might mess up Mr. McDougall's greenhouse looking for socks." He pulled on Dad's arm. "We have to go there and get the truck to bring Fluffy and Stanley back!"

When they got there, the greenhouse was dark, and there was no truck in sight.

Chapter 18

At the thought of what the plants might do while searching for nonexistent socks, Dad decided, "We'll go home and look up McDougall's home number and call him to meet us back here so we can get the plants."

Michael suggested, "Maybe one of the helpers could still be in there."

"I don't think so," said Dad. "But we might as well try knocking on the door."

When they got out of the car, Norman ran ahead.

"Some glass in the door is broken," he said.

"Be very quiet," Dad warned. He took a close look. A pane of glass next to the door handle had been smashed. The door was unlocked.

"There's been a break-in," said Dad.

Michael, thinking about Wanda Curly, asked, "Could it be a break-*out*?"

"No," said Dad. "If the glass was broken from the

inside, some of the pieces would have fallen outside. We have to call the police.''

Michael said, ''There's a phone on the counter right inside the door.''

Norman said, ''I'm worried about Fluffy. And Stanley and Curly, too.'' He pushed the door open far enough to stick his head in.

Dad silently gestured to the boys to follow him to the car. As he led the way, he whispered, ''The intruders may still be in there. We'll go find the nearest phone.'' When he looked behind him, Michael was there. But Norman was not. In the bright moonlight, they could not see him anywhere. He had slipped through the door into the greenhouse.

Dad and Michael ran back to the door. Dad stuck his head in and whispered, ''Norman, come out of there. Right now.'' There was no answer. ''Don't make me come in after you,'' warned Dad. They stood still and listened. The greenhouse was silent except for the far-off sound of water dripping.

''Now we'll have to use the phone here,'' Dad told Michael. ''You call 911 while I go after Norman. We have to get him out immediately in case anybody else might be in there.''

They stepped inside quietly. The moon shone through the glass roof, making it easy to see clearly, but everything looked eerie in the silvery light.

As Michael turned toward the counter, clouds swept in front of the moon. Suddenly there was total darkness. He wanted to find the door and get out. But he heard Dad faintly whispering Norman's name and realized he had already moved far down the main aisle. He also heard a few thumps and clunks as Dad bumped into things in the dark.

Michael stretched his arms out and shuffled toward the counter until he bumped into it. He felt around for the phone.

Norman had hurried into the greenhouse thinking Dad and Michael would be right behind him. When Dad said they should call the police, Norman had thought he meant he would go in to use the greenhouse phone.

He was hurrying along whispering Fluffy's name and listening for leaves to rustle in reply. He had gone quite far into the greenhouse before he realized that neither Dad nor Michael was following. He had stopped, wondering whether he should go back, when everything went dark. Now he heard someone whispering far off, "Norman. Norman." As he opened his mouth to answer, he heard other voices, not whispering. There were three guys somewhere up ahead in the dark. They sounded like teenagers.

One said, "This is a great place. Plenty of glass to smash! I found a back door, in case we need to get out of here in a hurry."

Another said, "Until the moon comes back out, we can't see where we're going. Why didn't one of you bring a flashlight? I put my paint can down and now I can't find it."

"Don't spray it in the dark. You might get it on me," said another, laughing. "I don't look good in purple."

"I've got some yellow, too. You'd look good in that 'cause you're so chicken. *Cluck, cluck, cluck.* You didn't want to break in here."

111

"I just said people might see us through the glass walls."

"Well, nobody can see us right now, including us. This is boring just hanging around in the dark."

"Hey, did you hear a noise?"

"Yeah, water dripping."

"Not that. More like leaves rustling."

"No, but the place is full of plants. Leaves could be moving. Maybe some of the big plants are monsters. They're coming to get you. Ha! Ha!"

"We can attack them with the paint. Monster plants would look good purple or yellow."

The vandals burst out laughing. Then they were quiet for a few moments.

"Did you hear something?" one asked.

"Yeah, monster plants creeping up behind us. Ooooh, I'm so scared."

"No, really. I thought I heard something—sort of like a whisper. It sounded like 'uffy' or maybe 'luffy.' "

"It's a monster plant whispering to you. To lure you to your doom in the dark. Don't worry, we won't let it get you. *Cluck, cluck, cluck.*"

"Shut up!"

"Cluck, cluck, cluck."

"Be quiet. I definitely heard something."

"I did, too."

"It couldn't be, but it sounds like skateboard wheels. There it is again. It's getting closer. Now it stopped."

The moon came out from behind the clouds. Its light shone brightly through the glass roof again.

Norman ducked down behind some plants and peeked

out. He saw three guys. A couple of them were holding small crowbars. They began smashing glass.

Now that Michael could see what he was doing, he found the phone, ducked behind the counter, and dialed 911. He told the dispatcher what was happening.

"Stay on the line," she instructed. Michael clutched the phone and wondered where Dad, Norman, Stanley, and Fluffy were.

The vandals were making so much noise smashing glass and whooping and hollering that Norman didn't worry about them hearing him. Whispering, "Fluffy, Fluffy," he crawled on. Many aisles away, Dad began running, searching around every corner for Norman.

"It's the night of the full moon," shouted one of the vandals. "Perfect for werewolves!" They began howling and laughing.

"Here's my paint," said another. "And here's some big garden tools. Great for smashing."

"Hey, before the moon went behind the clouds, did you notice if these two big plants were standing here?"

"No, but they had to be," replied another. "Plants can't walk around."

"OOOOO-EEEE," wailed the other one eerily. "Maybe monster plants can walk. They're coming after you."

"Wait a minute. These are sitting on skateboards. They must have been what I heard."

"You must have bumped into them in the dark and moved them."

"I didn't bump into anything that felt leafy."

"Let's play tic-tac-toe with these panes. Me first." *Smash.* "Your turn."

113

"No fair, you always go first and take the middle square." More smashes.

"I win!"

"Now it's my turn to go first." *Smash.*

Michael told the dispatcher that a lot of glass smashing was going on. He hoped the police would get there right now. If they didn't, the vandals would have most of Mr. McDougall's building smashed pretty soon.

Norman, who was close to the vandals, heard something rattling. He recognized the sound. Someone was shaking a can of spray paint, getting ready to use it.

"Let's paint this whole bunch of plants. These big ones would look good purple." The can rattled again. Norman felt a surge of anger. Paint would hurt Fluffy and Stanley and the other plants or even kill them. He had to do something. What the sensay had taught him popped into his mind. He could use karate to defend loved ones being attacked! As he heard the spray paint hiss, he took a deep breath and burst out of hiding.

"Hi! Ah!" he yelled and charged at a gallop. The surprised vandals turned around to see what was coming at them. Their looks of fear turned to amazement.

Norman ran right into the one holding the paint and caught him off balance. He toppled over, dropping the can.

Norman stopped with his fists up in a karate stance.

"Don't hurt those plants!" he commanded. "And stop breaking Mr. McDougall's glass!"

"It's just a kid!" exclaimed one of the vandals. "Where'd you come from, shorty?"

The fallen vandal was crawling around, looking for his paint can.

114

"Leave all the plants alone," shouted Norman. "Or I'll make you! Watch out! I take karate!"

One of the vandals laughed.

"Be careful," warned the one on the floor. "He knocked me down. And I hear somebody else running this way. If they know we're here, they must have called the police. Let's get out of here! Does anybody see my paint can?"

From around a corner came Mr. McDougall's wheelchair, speeding with Wanda Curly at the controls. She rammed the chair into two vandals standing together. Boom! As they teetered and were falling over, clouds covered the moon again. The greenhouse was plunged into total darkness.

"What was that?" said one of the vandals, sounding like he was on the floor.

The next sound was a loud *hisssss*. Oh, no, thought Norman, the guy found the can. He's spraying the plants.

Somebody said, "Yuck! What's happening?"

Then Norman heard a whirr, like a little motor. In the next instant there was a blinding flash of light. It lit up the scene as if the sun had suddenly come out. That lasted only a moment. There was total darkness again. But the light had lasted long enough for Norman to see what was happening.

Chapter 19

Fluffy was holding the spray can. One of the vandals on the floor now had purple hair. One still standing had a big splat of purple on the front of his shirt. Stanley was holding the missing camera. And Wanda Curly was backing up to make another run as if the vandals were bowling pins she was planning to knock over.

In the dark Dad shouted angrily, "Leave my son alone!"

"Leave *him* alone?" protested a vandal. "Tell him and his robot plants—or whatever they are—to leave *us* alone!

Norman yelled, "They're monster plants. They're coming to get you! And they know karate!" The spray can hissed again and again.

Stanley took another flash picture that lit up the dark. The vandals looked almost completely purple now. Wanda Curly was speeding toward them. In the moment of light, they saw her and jumped out of the way.

"Run for the back door," yelled one.

"I can't see to run anywhere," yelled another.

"Run anyway!"

There were many thuds and bangs in the dark as the vandals bumped and tripped along, frantically trying to find the back door. Norman and Dad stayed put. Norman hoped Fluffy and Stanley were staying put, too, so they wouldn't get hurt.

Dad bumped into Norman and put his arms around him. "Don't worry," he said. "The police should be here soon."

"The camera isn't lost anymore," said Norman. "Stanley's got it."

"I'm not worried about the camera right now," said Dad.

Stanley flashed the camera again, showing that he and Fluffy were standing nearby. Wanda Curly was parked next to them in the wheelchair.

"They're okay," said Norman.

Suddenly the clouds passed, and moonlight flooded in again.

The vandals started yelling at each other about which way to go, now that they could see where they were going.

Wanda Curly started rolling away. Stanley and Fluffy grabbed on to the back of the wheelchair to go along for the ride.

"Stop!" called Norman. He went after them. Wanda Curly picked up speed.

The plants were really rolling when they got near the back door. One vandal was trying to figure out now to unlock the door for their getaway.

Wanda Curly bumped one of them hard against the climbing rose by the door. Thorns caught him, scratching and clawing his arms and hands and hooking into his clothes.

"Ow!" he yelled as he struggled to get loose. "Ow! Ow! Ow!" The thorns held on.

One of the two still trying to get out the door made a move to run in the other direction.

Norman called, "Fluffy!" and sang, "Put your right vine in! Hi! Ah!" Fluffy lashed out a vine and knocked the fleeing vandal into a group of cactuses. The teenager pulled away with both hands and arms stuck full of sharp spines.

"Ow! Ow!" he said, trying to pull them out.

Fluffy pressed his vines to his sides and bowed.

Only one vandal made it out the back door, right into the thorny bushes and stinging nettles. At that moment the police came running from both directions—outside toward the back door and inside from the front of the greenhouse, with Michael trailing.

"Freeze! Don't move!" they yelled.

"I can't move," said the vandal caught by the bushes. "Get these plants off me!"

An officer inspected him with his flashlight. "I hate to have to tell you this," he said, "since you've gone to so much trouble to paint yourself purple, but you're several months too early for Halloween."

Dad hugged Norman. Norman bowed to Fluffy and said, "Arigato!" Fluffy bowed back. Michael patted Stanley's leaves. Stanley handed him the camera. Then Fluffy, Stanley, and Wanda Curly slapped their vines

118

together, as if they were giving each other high fives. Michael took their picture.

The police rescued the vandals from the painful clutches of the rose and thorny bushes and took them away in handcuffs. As police cars were leaving, Mom and the Sparkses arrived in the van.

"When we got home and you weren't there," Mom said, "I kept calling the greenhouse, but the line was always busy. We decided to come over and see if everything was all right. Were Fluffy and Stanley acting up?"

"No," replied Norman. "They helped catch the vandals who've been spray painting and wrecking things. And Wanda Curly helped, too. She was great!" He told everybody what had happened.

Dr. Sparks said she'd better take Wanda Curly back to the house for the night instead of leaving her at the greenhouse until morning. "I'll stay up and watch her, so she won't cause any problems," she said.

Michael told Sarah, "She did wonderful things. Norman said she was amazing."

Sarah said, "Wanda Curly is the best. She deserves a blue ribbon, but all I've got is a red one." She took off her hair ribbon and tied it in a pretty bow around the plant's top curly vine.

Dr. Sparks remarked, "The research with this plant is going to be interesting."

Mr. McDougall arrived soon after police called him. He got Wanda Curly out of his wheelchair so he could use it to get around faster. His employees arrived to help secure the greenhouse.

The Sparkses took Wanda Curly back to the house in the van. Mom drove Dad's car. Dad and the boys

119

walked Stanley and Fluffy home. The evening had grown chilly, and they hurried along.

Dad remarked, "It really is beautiful out tonight with the moonlight."

"A good night for werewolves," said Norman. He gave a couple of wolf howls.

"Stop that," said Dad.

Michael said, "His howling sounds better than his singing."

So Norman began to sing, off-key as usual: "Oh Susanna, oh, don't you cry for me. I'm going to Lew-see-anna with a banjo on my kneeeeeeeee!"

"Oh, yuck," said Michael.

As Fluffy and Stanley rolled along, they waved a few vines in time to Norman's song.

Chapter 20

When they got home, it was past their bedtime. Max was already asleep in his sleeping bag in Mom and Dad's room, where his parents were going to spend the night. Sarah was going to sleep in there, too. Mom and Dad were taking the boys' room. Wanda Curly was sitting on the coffee table. Michael and Norman brought their plants and sleeping bags into the living room.

Dr. Sparks said, "I'm going to stay up and watch all three plants tonight." She went to change clothes and get her notebook.

Sarah came in to look at Curly. She fiddled with the ribbon to make the bow look better.

Michael opened the plastic bag that held half of Stanley's meal and put the white socks with brown stripes on the floor. He took off his brown socks and added them to the heap.

"Fudge ripple tonight, Stanley," he said, showing off because Sarah was there. "And chocolate for dessert."

Sarah wrinkled her nose. "Just fudge ripple and chocolate? Your plants are vegetarians. That's not a well-balanced meal for vegetarians—or any other kind of eaters."

"Actually," Michael replied, "they're socketarians."

Sarah giggled. "You still should feed them more nutritious socks—fruit and vegetable-colored ones—like lemon and watermelon and carrots and broccoli."

"Nope," said Michael. "I have to wear them first to get them smelly. I'm not wearing yellow or pink or orange or green socks."

"How about grape?" suggested Sarah.

Michael scrunched up his face at the thought of wearing purple socks.

"Cauliflower?" said Sarah.

Michael said, "Maybe. I guess white with no stripes would be okay. But that's also vanilla. Stanley likes vanilla. But if I told him it was cauliflower, he might not like it."

They started laughing and calling out fruits and vegetables.

"Squash!" said Sarah.

"Cantaloupe!" said Michael.

"Tomatoes!"

"Celery!"

"Bananas!"

"Potatoes!"

"Green beans!"

"Asparagus!"

Mom came in. "What is this?" she asked. "Dueling vegetables?"

This only made Sarah and Michael laugh harder.

Mom said, "Sarah, it's your turn for the bathroom." Sarah went down the hall, still laughing. They heard the bathroom door close. Dad and Norman came into the living room.

"What's so funny?" asked Dad.

Michael stopped laughing long enough to reply, "It's hard to explain."

They heard the bathroom door open. Sarah yelled, "Eggplants!" and slammed the door.

Michael burst out laughing again. Norman laughed, too.

"What's so funny about eggplants?" asked Dad.

Norman said, "I thought she said 'egg*pants*.' Like eggs wearing pants. That's funny. But I don't think eggplants are funny."

Mom said, "They *are* one of the funniest looking vegetables."

"Why are they called eggplants?" wondered Norman.

"I don't know," said Dad. "We'll look it up in the morning."

Norman thought for a moment. Then he asked, "Plants don't lay eggs. Do they?"

"Not that we know of," replied Dad. "But with plants, I'm beginning to think anything is possible."

Norman checked with Dr. Sparks. She assured him that although many insects lay their eggs on or inside plants, there are no plants that lay eggs themselves—at least none discovered so far.

* * *

After everyone else went to sleep, Dr. Sparks curled up on the couch with her notebook. She watched Fluffy and Stanley schlurp and burp. She saw Stanley politely offer to share some of his dinner with Wanda Curly. He poked a chocolate sock at her, but she wasn't interested.

The plants didn't do anything else. Dr. Sparks thought they must be tired from all they had been through. She yawned and tried to keep her eyes open. Nothing else would probably happen tonight. She gave up watching and went to bed.

After a while, Stanley found the TV remote. He flicked from channel to channel. The noise was not loud enough to wake the boys.

Finally, Stanley found a nature program and stopped changing channels. He rolled closer to the coffee table, where Wanda Curly sat.

Together they enjoyed the program, holding vines.

The Sparkses left early the next morning. The boys stood with Dad and Mom in the driveway, waving good-bye. The last they saw of Wanda Curly was her red ribbon, bobbing in the back window of the van as it drove away.

Chapter 21

Things got back to normal—or as normal as they ever could be in a family that included Stanley, Fluffy, and Norman. That night everyone was glad to be back in their own beds and slept soundly. Stanley found the camera again. He took more pictures, but the flash did not wake anyone up.

Early in the morning Norman and Fluffy practiced their karate moves together quietly. Norman went to the kitchen before Mom got there. When he opened the refrigerator to get juice, he was surprised to find a shopping bag full of socks Mom had bought for plant food the day before. He knew she wouldn't have put it there. It must have been Fluffy or Stanley. He took the bag out. He was glad he had discovered it before Mom did.

At breakfast Dad asked Mom, "Did you drop off the film to be developed yesterday?"

"No, I thought the roll wasn't finished yet."

"We should get it developed now anyway," said Dad. "We need to give the police any shots that Stanley might have gotten of the vandals. We don't have to mention exactly who took them." He got the camera and looked to see how many pictures had been taken. But the roll *was* finished. He took it out. "I'll drop this off on my lunch hour today," he said.

"Get double prints," Mom reminded him.

School was going well for Michael that day until recess. He was talking to Chad and Brad as usual when he saw Kim and Pat heading toward them from the far side of the playground.

Oh, no, he thought. Pat Jenkins had finally gotten up the nerve to tell him she liked him. In his mind, as she came closer and closer, he heard the theme music from *Jaws.* Then he tried not to think the worst. Maybe he would luck out. Maybe they were coming over because Kim had decided that this week she liked Brad or Chad. That would be okay.

The girls stopped in front of them. Pat Jenkins said, "I like you"—to Brad.

"Oh," said Brad, developing a sudden interest in his shoelaces. "That's nice." The girls hurried away, giggling.

Chad elbowed Brad. "Pat Jenkins likes you!" he teased.

Brad replied, "I could sort of like her. She always has cool stuff to trade in her lunch."

Michael felt annoyed. Pat liked Brad? Then why was she always talking to Michael if she didn't like him? He wondered if he would ever understand girls.

*　　*　　*

126

When Dad brought the developed pictures home, the family gathered around to look at them. The auction party photos Mom and Dad had taken turned out well. The greenhouse photos included three of the vandals. The first showed them holding crowbars. In the second, they were partly purple, and in the third, completely purple. The rest of the pictures were a surprise.

"Uh-oh," said Michael. "I think Stanley got hold of the camera again."

These pictures had obviously been taken at home in the middle of the night. Fluffy was pulling Norman's covers up to his chin.

"I didn't know he did that," said Norman.

Michael was asleep in his bed with his face lying sideways on an open book and a flashlight in his hand.

"Hmmm," said Mom. "I thought you weren't doing that any more."

"It was a really good book," explained Michael.

Next Stanley had gone across the hall to Mom and Dad's room. Dad was asleep with his mouth wide open, looking very funny.

"Oh, no," he said. He tore up the picture.

Mom waved another one. "Double prints," she said, laughing. "I'll save this one for blackmail the next time you don't want to go shopping with me." Dad burst out laughing, too.

"Then I'll blackmail you back with this one," he said. Mom was asleep with her face lying sideways on an open book and a flashlight in her hand.

"Well," she said sheepishly, "it was a very good book!"

"Why were you using a flashlight?" asked Dad. "Why didn't you turn on your bedside lamp?"

"I knew it would wake you up," she explained. "You would have asked me to turn it off so you could sleep."

Michael asked, "How come you can do that when I'm not supposed to?"

"Because I'm a grown-up. Grown-ups can stay up later than children."

"No fair," said Michael.

"When you're a grown-up," said Mom, "you can stay up as late as you want." She laughed. "And sleep with your mouth open, too."

"Sometimes he already sleeps with his mouth open," said Norman.

The last two pictures showed Fluffy opening the refrigerator door and putting a shopping bag inside.

"What was he doing?" asked Dad.

Mom said, "That's a bag from the Save-A-Lot Discount Store. I bought a supply of socks there the other day. Why would Fluffy put socks in the fridge?"

"He wanted cold socks?" asked Norman.

Michael said, "Maybe he was trying to make them into Popsicles."

Norman exclaimed, "He was inventing a new food! Socksicles! We could make tons of money with those!"

Dad said, "That's certainly a creative idea, but I don't think socksicles would catch on too well with humans. Fluffy and Stanley would probably be the only customers."

A few days later, when the boys got home from school, Mom looked through the mail that had just been delivered.

"Here's something interesting," she said. "A letter addressed to Stanley. The return address on the envelope belongs to the Sparkses, but the name is W.C. Temple."

"Wanda Curly wrote Stanley a letter?" Norman said. He grabbed for it, but Michael got it first and ripped it open.

"It's to *my* plant, so I get to read it," he said.

Norman hung over his shoulder. "I want to see what plant writing looks like," he said.

Michael unfolded the letter. A little snippet of red ribbon fell out. "It's people writing," he said, "but it's in green ink."

He read aloud:

"Dear Stanley,

I am fine. How are you? I like living here. They don't have any wheelchairs. So I don't go out of the Sparkses' home greenhouse by myself. I like the other plants here. I have many new friends. Sometimes Dr. Sparks gives me rides in the van to the research center. I don't get bored. It is nice here. Did you take any more pictures? If you did, send me one. Are you eating healthy socks? Don't eat too many fudge ripples. Say hi to Fluffy and Norman and Michael for me. Write back.

Your friend,
Wanda Curly"

Mom looked at the letter. "Sarah must have written all this down for Wanda Curly," she told Michael. "Are you going to write back?"

He replied, "Maybe Stanley will."

Michael waited a few days before starting to answer the letter. His first try turned out to be a rough draft because he kept crossing things out and thinking of new things to put in. He revised it four times. It took him a week. When he was finished, he copied it over because the first time it didn't look neat enough.

Dear Wanda Curly,

I am fine. How are you? Nothing big has happened here since you left. The police don't come by any more. Fluffy hasn't spray painted anybody purple lately. Maybe that is because he is not allowed to have any spray paint. Sometimes I wish I had spray paint to use on Norman when he gets up early and practices karate with Fluffy. Fluffy put a bag of new socks in the refrigerator. Norman thinks he was trying to make socksickles. Here is a picture of Fluffy doing it. (We got double prints.) I took this picture. I hope you are having fun.

Your friend,
Stanley

Michael thought a moment and added one more thing:

P.S. Write back.